AN UNLIKELY BRIDE FOR THE BILLIONAIRE

BY
MICHELLE DOUGLAS

MILLS
BOON

Published in Great Britain 2016
By Mills & Boon, an imprint of HarperCollins*Publishers*
1 London Bridge Street, London, SE1 9GF

© 2016 Michelle Douglas

ISBN: 978-0-263-06507-7

'The girl in that photograph is the woman you're meant to be. I know it and you know it.'

He was wrong! She *didn't* deserve to be that girl. She deserved nothing more than the chance to live her life in peace.

His breath fanned across her lips, addling her brain. She should step away, but she remained, quivering beneath his touch, hardly knowing what she wished for.

He pressed a kiss to the corner of her mouth. Her eyes fluttered closed as she turned towards him…

And then she found herself released.

'You want me as much as I want you.'

Her heart thudded in her chest. She had to reach out and steady herself against a chair.

'I don't know why the thought of being happy scares you.'

Dear Reader,

This story has been percolating away in my mind for a while. It all started when I heard the song 'Tie a Yellow Ribbon Round the Ole Oak Tree' twice in the same week. It's a song my grandma used to sing, but other than the chorus I'm not sure I'd ever paid attention to the lyrics before… So I blinked when I realised the singer/narrator of the song was returning home after three years in prison.

What?

Of course this engaged my writing brain immediately. In odd moments I'd start playing with different scenarios and trying to answer the questions that arose—how had he ended up in prison? What did he want now? How would he deal with the guilt and shame…or would he be angry and bitter? Would he find it hard to adjust in the real world after prison? What if my ex-convict wasn't a he but a she?

And that is how Mia and Dylan's story was born. It's a story of redemption and forgiveness, a story of moving beyond one's past and trusting the future— and, Dear Reader, it's a story of love.

I hope you enjoy Mia and Dylan's journey towards their happy-ever-after. And I hope you come to love them as much as I do.

Hugs,

Michelle

Michelle Douglas has been writing for Mills & Boon since 2007, and believes she has the best job in the world. She lives in a leafy suburb of Newcastle, on Australia's east coast, with her own romantic hero, a house full of dust and books, and an eclectic collection of '60s and '70s vinyl. She loves to hear from readers and can be contacted via her website: michelle-douglas.com.

Visit the Author Profile page at millsandboon.co.uk for more titles.

To Amber and Anthony, and Jessica and Tim,
who are raising the next generation of
heroes and heroines with grace and style…
and a splendid sense of fun!

CHAPTER ONE

'BUT—' MIA STARED, aghast, at Gordon Coulter '—that's not my job!' She was a trainee field officer, not a trainee event manager.

Her stomach performed a slow, sickening somersault at the spiteful smile that touched his lips. Gordon was the council administrator in charge of Newcastle's parks and wildlife—her boss's boss and a petty bureaucrat to boot. Plum Pines Reserve fell under his control. And he'd made no secret of the fact that he'd love to get rid of her—that he was simply waiting for her to mess up so he could do exactly that.

She did her best to moderate her voice. 'I'm in charge of the weed extermination project that's to start on the eastern boundary. Veronica—' the reserve's ranger '—insists it's vital we get that underway as soon as possible. We're supposed to be starting today.'

'Which is why I've handed that project over to Simon.'

Every muscle stiffened in protest, but Mia bit back the objections pressing against the back of her throat. She'd worked ridiculously hard on fine-tuning that project, had gathered together an enthusiastic band of volunteers who didn't care one jot about her background. More exciting still, she and Veronica had planned to take a full botanical inventory of the area—a comprehensive project that had filled Mia with enthusiasm. And now she was to have no part in it.

'This isn't up for debate, Mia.'

Gordon pursed his lips, lifting himself up to his full paunchy height of five feet ten inches. If it was supposed to make him look impressive, it failed. It only drew her attention to the damp half-moons at the armpits of his business shirt.

'You have to understand that teamwork is vital in an area as poorly funded as ours. If you're refusing to assist the administrative team in their hour of need then perhaps this isn't the right organisation for you.'

She wanted to know where Nora was. She wanted to know why Simon hadn't been given *this* job instead of her.

'The Fairweathers will be here at any moment, so if you *are* refusing to assist...'

'Of course I'm not refusing.' She tried to keep her voice level. She couldn't afford to lose this job. 'I'm surprised you'd trust me with such an important assignment, that's all.'

His eyes narrowed. 'If you screw this up, Maydew, you'll be out on your ear.'

She didn't doubt that for a moment.

'Naturally Nora will take over once she returns.' His lips tightened. 'She assures me you're the only one who can possibly deputise in her stead.'

She bit back a sigh. Nora wanted her on the events team, claiming she was wasted as a field officer. Mia had plans, though, and they didn't involve being part of the events team.

Where was Nora?

She didn't ask. She refused to give Gordon the satisfaction of telling her it was none of her business. She'd ring Nora later and make sure she was okay.

The receptionist knocked on the office door. It was Nora's office, but Gordon co-opted it whenever he decided to work from Plum Pines rather than his office at Council Chambers.

'Mr Coulter? Mr Fairweather is here.'

'Send him in.'

Mia moved to the side of the desk—she hadn't been invited to sit—fighting the urge to move to the back of the room, where she'd be able to remain as unobtrusive as possible.

'Mr Fairweather, it's delightful to meet you!' Gordon moved forward, arm outstretched, greasy smile in place.

Mia repressed a shudder.

And then she glanced at Dylan Fairweather—and had to blink, momentarily dazzled by so much golden...*goldenness*. Dear Lord, the papers did Dylan Fairweather no justice whatsoever. Not that Mia spent much time reading the society pages, but even *she*—hermit that she was—knew that Dylan Fairweather was considered one of Australia's bright young things. Earlier in the year he'd been named one of Australia's Top Twenty Eligible Bachelors.

If steal-your-breath sex appeal was one of the criteria then Dylan Fairweather had that in spades! Too-long dark gold hair and sexy designer stubble coupled with a golden tan had Mia's fingers curling into her palms. At six feet two he towered over Gordon, his pale blue business shirt and sand-coloured chinos achieving a casual elegance Gordon had no hope of matching.

Nor did his clothes hide the breadth of his shoulders or the latent strength of powerful thighs. All that power and flaxen golden brilliance should have made him look terrifying—like a prowling lion. But it didn't. He looked...he looked like a prince out of a fairytale.

Mia tried to tear her gaze away, but couldn't. Never, in all of her twenty-five years, had she been in the presence of someone so physically perfect.. She remembered one of the women in prison describing how she'd felt when she'd first laid eyes on Vincent van Gogh's painting *The Starry Night*. That was how Mia felt now.

Swallowing, she shook herself, appalled at the way her heart raced, at the craving that clawed at her belly. Pulling in a breath, she reminded herself that she wasn't some primitive savage, controlled by greed and impetuous impulses. Not any more.

When Gordon had said she'd be taking care of the Fair-weathers today, she'd been expecting a blushing bride and her aunt, maybe an attendant or two. She hadn't been expecting the bride's *brother*.

His pleasantries with Gordon exchanged, he turned to her and offered his hand with an easy, 'Dylan Fairweather.'

She took it automatically, appreciating the just-firm-enough grip and almost melting under the unexpected warmth of his smile.

You're not the melting type.

'Mia Maydew. It's nice to meet you. Carla is taking a call. She should only be a moment.'

'That's no problem at all.' Gordon ushered Dylan to a chair, frowning at Mia over his head.

Dear God! Had her paralysing preoccupation been evident for all to see? Heat climbed into her face. Brilliant. Just brilliant.

Gordon took his chair. He still didn't invite Mia to sit. 'Unfortunately Nora can't join us today. She sends her apologies. She was involved in a car accident on her way to work this morning.'

Mia couldn't prevent her involuntary intake of breath, or the way her hand flew to her abdomen, just below her breasts, to counter the way her stomach jumped. Startlingly brilliant blue eyes surveyed her for a moment, and while the brilliant colour might have the ability to distract a mere mortal, Mia sensed the shrewdness behind them.

Dylan Fairweather shifted ever so slightly on his chair. 'I hope she's okay.'

'Yes, yes, she's fine, but her car is apparently a write-off. I insisted she go to the hospital for a thorough examination, though.'

Mia closed her eyes briefly and let out a breath.

'Wise,' agreed Dylan—*Mr Fairweather*.

'In her stead—as a temporary measure, you understand—you'll have Mia here to run you through wedding options.

Anything you'd like to know—ask her. Anything you'd like to see—she'll show it to you. I promise that nothing will be too much trouble.'

Easy for him to say.

She straightened. It wasn't the Fairweathers' fault that Gordon had thrust her into the role of Assistant Events Manager. She'd helped Nora out before with weddings and corporate events. She'd do everything she could to answer the Fairweathers' questions and help Carla plan the wedding of her dreams.

'If you'd like to take it from here, Mia?'

'Certainly.' She forced a noncommittal smile to her face. 'If you'd just hand me the Fairweather file from the top drawer of the desk, I'll take Mr Fairweather through to the meeting room.'

She was tempted to laugh at the disgruntled expression that flitted across Gordon's face. Had he really thought she didn't know about the file? She'd helped Nora compile parts of it earlier in the week. Did he hate her so much that he'd risk a lucrative account, not to mention some seriously good publicity, to undermine her? The thought killed any urge to smile.

She had to counsel herself to take the file calmly, before leading Dylan Fairweather out of the office to the meeting room. Her pulse skittered and perspiration gathered at her nape. She preferred working with animals to people. Better yet, she liked working with plants. With over one hundred and seventy hectares of natural bushland to its name, it should have been relatively easy to avoid human contact at Plum Pines Reserve.

'Can I get you tea or coffee…maybe some water?' She gestured for Dylan to take a chair at the table, doing what she could to stop her fingers from shaking. This account had excited Nora enormously and, Gordon aside, Mia wanted to do her best for her boss.

From across the table Dylan eyed her closely, a frown in

his eyes, although his lips remained curved upwards in a pleasant smile. 'I think a carafe of water and three glasses would be an excellent idea.'

He thought *she* needed a drink of water? Dear Lord. She scurried away to fetch it. Did her nerves show that badly? She usually came across as a difficult study. She took a couple of deep breaths to compose herself before returning to the meeting room.

'Nora is a friend of yours?' he asked when she was seated, taking charge of the carafe and pouring a glass of water before pushing it across the table to her.

It hit her then that he'd misread her nerves as worry for the other woman. She hesitated. Would Nora consider Mia a friend? 'Nora is a close colleague. I like her a lot.'

'The news of her accident was a shock?'

She wasn't used to anyone being interested in her reactions. 'It was. I'm relieved it's not too serious.' When he continued to stare at her—which did nothing to slow her heart-rate—she forced her lips upwards. 'I'll call her later to check if there's anything she needs. It's kind of you to be so concerned. Now, let me show you the material Nora and I have gathered in relation to Ms Fairweather's wedding.'

'Please—you must call us Carla and Dylan.'

Must she? There was a certain protection afforded by the formality of Mr and Ms.

The customer is always right.

She bit back a sigh. If that were the case…

'Dylan.' She tested the name on her tongue. It emerged without any effort at all and tasted like her favourite brand of dark chocolate—flavoured with a bite of sea salt. His smile was her reward, making her forget the rest of her sentence.

'See…it wasn't so hard, was it—Mia?'

He made her name sound like a song.

He smiled. 'I can see why Carla requested you work on her wedding'

She opened her mouth and then closed it, blinking. 'I

think you've mistaken me for someone else. I'm afraid I don't know your sister, Mr Fair—uh... Dylan.'

He stared across at her, but in the end he merely nodded and let it go without challenge. It was as if someone had cut a string and released her.

She glanced down at the folder in an effort to collect herself. 'Do you know...?' She cleared her throat. 'Do you know where Carla would like the ceremony to take place?'

He glanced towards the door, as if hoping his sister would magically appear. 'Beside some lily pond. It's apparently where she and Thierry met.'

Right. Mia jotted a note down on her pad.

Blue eyes twinkled across the table at her when she looked up at him again. 'Aren't you going to gush about how romantic that is?'

Should she? Was gushing part of the job description?

He laughed as if he'd read that thought in her face, pointing a lean tanned finger at her. 'You, Ms Maydew, are *not* a romantic.'

He stared at her as if he knew her. It was utterly disconcerting. She had no intention of letting him know that, though.

She pointed her pen back at him. 'I *am*, however, an excellent worker.'

'Perfect.' His grin widened. 'You'll at least provide a port of sanity amid all the craziness.'

That made her lips twitch. She'd watched TV programs about Bridezillas. Was that what they had on their hands with Carla?

'Hallelujah!' He raised his hands heavenwards.

'What?'

'I finally managed to get a proper smile out of you.'

She stared at him, nonplussed. Why should he care one way or the other whether she smiled or not? Was smiling also part of the job description?

Darn it—it probably was! Give her animals and plants any day.

She forced her lips to curve upwards.

'Oh, dear me, no! On a scale of one to ten, that's not even going to score you a three.' He donned a mock commentator's voice. *'And Mia's smile has only scored a two point one from the Romanian judge!'*

She had to choke back a laugh.

He leant his elbows on the table. There was the whole width of the table between them, but somehow he seemed to bridge that distance without any effort at all. Maybe it was a combination of his height and breadth? She could make out the tiny laughter lines that fanned out from his eyes. She suspected Dylan laughed a lot. She noted the dusky eyelashes…ridiculously long and tipped with gold…and the firm fullness of his bottom lip. She'd bet he kissed a lot too. A pulse started up in the centre of her chest.

'I suspect, Mia Maydew, it'd be really something to make you laugh.'

She couldn't explain why, but she found herself jerking back as if he'd just propositioned her.

To cover her confusion, she folded her arms and narrowed her eyes. 'I have your number, Dylan Fairweather.' She used his full name in the same way he'd used hers. 'You're an incorrigible flirt. I suspect you can't help yourself.'

He raised his hands. 'Guilty as charged! But it's flirting without intent…just a bit of frivolous nonsense.'

His smile made her stomach tumble. 'Then why…?'

'Because it's fun.' His grin widened and she swore he had the devil in his eyes. 'Aren't you going to flirt back?'

She couldn't help it. She laughed.

Thank heavens! The woman *could* laugh.

Dylan sat back and let out a breath when the rather plain and schoolmistressy Mia momentarily transformed from uptight and ordinary-looking to mischievous imp. His gaze lingered on her mouth. He hadn't noticed how wide and generous it was earlier.

Since he'd witnessed her shock at learning of Nora's accident, and sensed her nerves at being thrust into the role of wedding co-ordinator, he'd wanted to put her at ease. Putting people at ease was his stock in trade. Mia might call it flirting, but it was nothing more than a bit of harmless fun designed to make her laugh and loosen up. And it had half worked—she'd laughed.

Having now seen Mia smile for real, though, he could see that she was neither plain nor schoolmistressy. It was just an attitude she cultivated. Interesting…

Nora had been ecstatic yesterday when he'd mentioned that they'd like Mia as part of their wedding team. Nora mightn't have known it, but she'd unwittingly supplied a glowing character reference for Mia. He sat back, resisting the urge to rub his eyes. He wanted everything associated with this wedding to be a joy for Carla. He meant to ensure it went without a hitch.

If only he could be certain the damn wedding should go ahead!

The walls of the glassed-in meeting room pressed in on him. He wanted to be outside and in the fresh air. *Now!* He wanted to be away from the fresh juniper berry scent of the woman opposite. It had his mind turning to black ski runs in St Moritz, with the wind tearing at his hair and the cold making him feel alive. Which was ridiculous. While he might be on leave, this was no holiday. Besides, if there'd been less frivolity in his life recently Carla might never have become embroiled with a man like Thierry.

Carla's happiness—that was what he had to focus on. 'Is the lily pond far? Can you show it to me?'

'You want to see the lily pond *now*?'

'Yes.'

'What about your sister?'

'She's on the phone to her intended. She could be hours. I'll text her so she'll know where to find us.'

Dutifully he pulled out his phone.

Mia taking me to lily pond. Meet there.

He held it out for her to see and then hit 'send'.

Without another word Mia led him out into the warm summer sunshine and he filled his lungs with eucalypt-scented air. The small office block sat on the edge of a rectangle of lush lawn that had to be at least two football fields long. Covered picnic tables marched down each of its sides, shaded by a variety of gum trees, plum pines and bottle-brush trees. The red blossoms of the bottlebrushes had attracted a flock of rainbow lorikeets which descended in a noisy colourful rush.

A peacock strutted through the nearest picnic shelter, checking for crumbs and leftovers, while a bush turkey raked through a nearby pile of leaves. All around the air was filled with birdcalls and the scent of warmed native grasses. Groups of people had gathered around the picnic tables and on blankets on the grass. He could hear children's laughter from the playground he glimpsed through the trees.

'This place is popular.'

She gestured that they should take a path to the left. 'It is.'

Her dark brown hair, pulled back into a severe ponytail, gleamed rich and russet in the bright light. She didn't wear a scrap of make-up. Not that she needed to. She had a perfect peaches and cream complexion that he hadn't appreciated under the strip lighting of the office.

He pulled his mind back to the matter at hand. 'Can we book the entire reserve for the wedding?'

'I'm afraid not. Plum Pines is a public park. What we *can* do, though, is rope off the area where your event is being held to keep the general public out.'

'Hmm...' He'd have to rethink the security firm he'd initially considered hiring. The wedding security would be a bigger job than he'd originally thought.

She glanced up, her gaze sharp. 'Is that going to be a problem?'

'Not if I hire a good security firm.'

'Let me know if you'd like any recommendations.' She led him across a bridge spanning a large pond. 'Officially the park is open from seven a.m. to seven p.m.'

He stared out at the expanse of water, noting several black swans sitting on the edge of the far bank. 'Is this the lily pond?'

'No, it's the duck pond.'

He glanced down into the water and blinked when a tortoise poked its small head out of the water. 'That…' He halted to point. 'That was…'

She glanced over the railing. 'A Common Longneck Tortoise. The pond is full of them.'

Hands on hips, he completed a full circle, taking in the surroundings. Plum Pines was undeniably pretty, and the native forest rising up all around them undeniably grand. He'd visited some of the most exotic places the world had to offer and yet he'd somehow missed experiencing what was in his own backyard.

'I can't believe we're in the middle of the second largest city in New South Wales. It feels as if we're in the middle of the bush.'

'Yes, we're very privileged.'

That was a rote reply if he'd ever heard one—trotted out for the benefit of visitors. What did Mia really think of the place? Did she love it or loathe it? Her lips were pursed into a prim line that had him itching to make her smile again.

'You'll need to apply to the council for an event licence that'll allow the wedding to extend beyond those hours. There shouldn't be any issue with that, though.'

She moved off again, with her no-nonsense stride, and

after another glance at where the tortoise had disappeared he set off after her.

'Have you had any weddings that *haven't* extended beyond seven p.m.?' All of the weddings he'd ever attended had kicked on into the wee small hours.

'There's been a trend for morning weddings with lunchtime receptions. So, yes.'

She was so serious. And literal. He found himself starting to laugh.

She glanced at him, a frown crinkling her forehead. 'What's so funny?'

'You're not so good at small talk, are you?'

Her face fell and she stuttered to a halt. 'You want small talk?'

That made him laugh again. 'How do you enforce the seven p.m. closing time?'

'We close the gates to the car parks. There's a hefty fine involved to have the gates opened. Our people, along with your security firm, will have a list of your guests' number plates so they can come and go as they please.'

'Right.'

'And, as Plum Pines is in the middle of suburbia, we don't get much foot traffic or many homeless people looking for a place to put up for the night.'

That was something, he supposed.

She consulted her notepad. 'Do you know how many guests the bride and groom are planning to invite?'

'Carla informs me that she wants "a small and intimate affair".'

That frown crinkled her brow again. 'Do you happen to know what your sister's idea of "small" might be?'

'I wouldn't have a clue.' He had no idea if Thierry came from a large family or not. The other man had closed up like a clam when Dylan had asked him about them. 'I can't say that I know what she means by "intimate" either.'

Mia nodded. 'I think we can guess that fairly accurately—it probably includes fairy lights strung all around the marquee and surrounding trees, white linen tablecloths with centrepieces involving ivy and candles, vintage china and a string quartet.'

'You don't sound like you approve.'

She swung to face him. 'Mr Fair— Dylan. It's not for me to approve or disapprove. It's Plum Pines' job to help Carla plan the wedding she wants.'

'But—' He broke off.

'What were you going to say?'

He read the thought that flashed through her eyes—*Gordon Coulter promised nothing would be too much trouble.*

'Dylan, I'll do my best to deliver whatever is needed.'

Her moss-green eyes stared back at him, earnest and steady, and he found himself needing to pull a breath of air into cramped lungs. 'I need you to be as committed to this wedding as Carla.'

'I'm committed—I can promise you that.' Her teeth worried at her bottom lip. 'But that's not what you meant, is it? You want me to be exuberant and…and bouncy.'

He winced, realising how absurd that sounded when uttered out loud. He just wanted to see her smile again. *That* was what this was all about—and it was pure nonsense on his part.

He rubbed his hand across his nape. 'I think of weddings and I think of joy and excitement and…and *joy.*'

He wanted Carla's life filled with joy—not just her wedding. A fist tightened about his chest. If Thierry hurt her he'd—

Mia moved into his field of vision, making him blink. 'There's a lot of behind-the-scenes work that needs doing to make a wedding successful.' She pointed her pen at him. 'Joy and excitement are all well and good, but I figure my job is to keep a level head.'

A level head? That was exactly what he needed.

'Don't you believe someone can be quietly enthusiastic?' she asked.

'Of course they can. I'm sorry.' He grimaced. 'It's the bride who's supposed to go loopy, right? Not her brother.'

One of those rare smiles peeped out, making his heart thump.

'You're excited for her.' Too soon she sobered again. 'I'm naturally quiet. It doesn't mean I'm not invested.'

'Whereas I'm naturally gregarious.' It was what made him so good at his job. 'I sometimes forget that not everyone else is.'

'Do you still want to see the lily pond?'

'Yes, please.' He spoke as gravely as she did. 'My seeing the lily pond is not dependent on you being exuberant.'

He could have sworn that her lips twitched—for the briefest of moments. It sent a rush of something warm and sweet surging through his veins. He was glad he'd had a chance to meet her on his own. Carla had spoken of her often enough to make his ears prick up. It had been a long time since Carla had made a new female friend.

The question he needed to answer now, though—was Carla more than just a job to Mia? He'd give his right arm for Carla to have a girlfriend with whom to plan her wedding. And whatever the two of them dreamed up—schemed up—he'd make happen.

When he glanced back he found Mia staring at a point beyond him. He swung around to see an emu enclosure... and an emu sitting on the ground in the dirt. He glanced back to find her chewing her lip. 'Is that emu okay?' They *did* sit down, right?

She hesitated. 'Do you mind...?' She gestured towards the fence.

'Not at all.'

'Hey, Charlie—come on, boy!' Mia rattled the fence and the emu turned to stare, but when he didn't otherwise move she pulled out her phone. 'Janis? It's Mia. Charlie is looking decidedly under the weather. Can you send someone out to check on him?' Her lips pressed together as she listened to the person at the other end. 'He's sitting down and not responding to my calls.' She listened some more. 'But—'

She huffed out a breath and he could see her mentally counting to five.

'Right. If that's the best you can do.' She snapped the phone shut and shoved it back into her pocket.

'You're worried about him?'

One slim shoulder lifted. 'Charlie's been hand-raised. He's a social bird. Normally he'd be over here, begging for a treat. Everyone who works here is fond of him.'

Dylan glanced across at the emu. 'You want to go and give him the once over?'

She glanced around, as if to check that no one had overheard him. 'Would you mind?'

'Not at all.'

'It should only take me a moment. I just want to make sure he doesn't have something caught around his legs. Discarded plastic bags are the bane of our existence—they seem to blow in from everywhere.'

'I don't mind at all.'

Besides, he wanted her full attention once Carla arrived. He wanted her focussed on wedding preparations—not worrying about Charlie the Emu.

She moved towards a gate in the fence and unlocked it with a key she fished out from one of the many pockets of her khaki cargo pants.

She glanced back at him apologetically. 'I have to ask you to remain on this side of the fence. It's actually against the law for me to take you in with me.'

'Believe me, I'm happy to stay on this side of the fence, but…' he glanced across at Charlie '…that emu is huge. What if he attacks you?'

He couldn't in all conscious just stand here and do nothing.

'He won't hurt me. I promise.'

'In that case I promise to stay on this side of the fence.'

Nevertheless, he found his heart pounding a little too hard as she slipped into the enclosure and made her way towards the giant bird. She ran a soothing hand down its neck, not in the least intimidated by its size. He reminded himself that she was trained to deal with these animals, but he didn't take his eyes from her.

Slipping her arms beneath the bird, she lifted it to its knees, and Dylan could see something wrapped tight around its ankles. The poor bird was completely tangled! He watched in admiration as she deftly unwound it, shoving the remnants into her pocket. The entire time she crooned soothingly to the emu, telling him what a good boy he was and how pretty he was. Charlie leaned into her as much as he could, trusting her completely.

Finally she placed her arms beneath him with a cheery, 'Up we come, Charlie.'

The emu gave a kind of strangled *beep* before a stream of something green and vicious-looking shot out of the back of him, splattering all over the front of Mia's shirt. Only then did the bird struggle fully to its feet and race off towards a water trough. Mia stumbled backwards, a comical look of surprise on her face. She turned towards Dylan, utterly crestfallen and...and covered in bird poop.

Dylan clapped a hand over his mouth to hold back a shout of laughter. *Don't laugh!* An awful lot of women he knew would have simply burst into tears. If he laughed and then she cried he'd have to comfort her...and then he'd end up with bird poop all over *him* too.

Mia didn't cry. She pushed her shoulders back and squelched back over to the gate in the fence with as much dignity as she could muster. Still, even *she* had to find it difficult to maintain a sense of dignity when she was covered in bird poop.

She lifted her chin, as if reading that thought in his face. 'As you can see, Charlie left me a little present for my pains.'

He swallowed, schooling his features. 'You did a very good deed, Mia.'

'The thing is, when an emu gets stressed, the stress can result in...' she glanced down at herself, her nose wrinkling '...diarrhoea.'

'God, I'm *so* glad those birds can't fly!'

The heartfelt words shot out of him, and Mia's lips started to twitch as if the funny side of the situation had finally hit her.

Dylan couldn't hold back his laughter any longer. 'I'm sorry, Mia. You deserve better, but the look on your face when it happened... It was priceless!'

She grinned, tentatively touching the front of her shirt. 'That rotten bird! Here I am, supposedly trying to impress you and your sister with our marvellous facilities...and now you're going to live in fear of projectile diarrhoea from the native animals!'

The sudden image that came to his mind made him roar until he was doubled over. Mia threw her head back and laughed right alongside him. She laughed with an uninhibited gusto that transformed her completely. He'd glimpsed the mischievous imp earlier, but now she seemed to come alive—as if her mirth had broken some dam wall—as if she were a desert suddenly blooming with wildflowers.

Dylan's heart surged against his ribs and for a moment all he could do was stare. 'You should do that more often, you know. Laugh. You're beautiful when you laugh.'

She glanced up at him, the laughter dying on her lips. Something in the air shimmered between them, making them both blink. Her gaze lowered momentarily to his lips, before she turned beetroot-red. Swinging away, she stumbled across to the tap that stood by the gate in the fence.

Heat pulsed through him. So...the serious Mia wasn't immune to his charms after all?

The next moment he silently swore. *Damn!* He deserved a giant kick to the seat of his pants. She'd accused him of flirting earlier—but he hadn't meant to give her the wrong impression. He didn't want her thinking anything could happen between them. All flirtation and teasing on his part was entirely without intent.

She knelt at the tap and scrubbed at her shirt with a piece of rag. She must keep a veritable tool shed of handiness in those cargo pants of hers.

He watched in silence as she washed the worst of the mess from her shirt. 'I have a handkerchief if you need it.'

'Thank you, but I think this is the best I'm going to manage until I can change my shirt. Shall we continue on to the lily pond?'

'Yes, please.'

She gestured towards the path. 'Do you mind if I ring the office to give them an update on Charlie?'

'Not at all.'

And just like that they withdrew back into reserved professionalism. But something new pounded through Dylan— a curiosity that hadn't been there before. What an intriguing paradox Mia was proving to be...a fascinating enigma.

Which you don't have time for.

With a sigh, he pushed thoughts of Mia from his mind and forced his attention back to the impending wedding. He had to focus on what really mattered. He couldn't let Carla down—not when she needed him.

CHAPTER TWO

THEY REACHED THE lily pond two minutes later. The moment Dylan clapped eyes on the enchanting glade he understood why Carla had fallen in love with it. True to its name, large green lily pads decorated a small but picturesque body of oval water. Native trees and shrubs curved around three of its sides. The fourth side opened out to a large circle of green lawn.

Mia pointed to that now. 'This area is large enough for our medium-sized marquee, which holds sixty guests comfortably. That leaves the area behind for the caterers to set up their tents and vans for the food.'

Carla chose that moment to come rushing up—which was just as well, as Dylan had found himself suddenly in danger of getting caught up on the way Mia's wet shirt clung to her chest.

Carla grinned at Mia—'Surprise!'—before taking Dylan's arm and jumping from one foot to the other. 'Isn't this just the most perfect spot?'

He glanced down at her—at her smile made radiant with her newfound happiness. 'It's lovely,' he agreed, resolve solidifying in his gut. This wedding had come out of left field, taking him completely by surprise. But if this was what Carla truly wanted, he meant to create the perfect wedding for her. 'Where's Thierry?'

A cloud passed across her face. 'Something's come up. He can't make it.'

That was the problem. Thierry. Dylan didn't like the man.

His sister had suffered enough misery in her life, and Dylan had every intention of protecting her from further heartache.

Carla moved towards Mia. 'Please tell me you're not cross with me.'

'So…you're not really Carly Smith, frequent visitor and keen student of environmentalism?'

Carla shook her head.

Mia glanced down at her notepad. 'With your background, I imagine you need to be careful with your privacy.'

Carla winced. 'Please tell me you don't hate me. You've been so kind. I love shadowing you when you're on duty for the wildlife displays. You never talk down to me or treat me like I'm stupid. Oh!' she added in a rush. 'And just so you know, I really *do* have a keen interest in the environment and conservation.'

Mia smiled. 'Of course I don't hate you.'

That smile made Dylan's skin tighten. When she smiled she wasn't plain. And when she laughed she was beautiful.

He pushed those thoughts away. They had no bearing on anything. Her smile told him what he needed to know—Mia genuinely liked his sister. *That* was what mattered.

'Right.' Mia consulted her notepad. 'I want to hear every tiny detail you have planned for this wedding.'

'Hasn't Dylan told you *anything*?'

Mia glanced at him. 'We didn't want to start without you.'

That was unexpectedly diplomatic.

He stood back while the pair started discussing wedding preparations, jumping from one topic to the next as if it made utterly logical sense to do so. He watched them and then shook his head. Had he really thought Carla needed exuberance from Mia? Thank heaven Mia had seen the wisdom in not trying to fake it. He silently blessed her tact in not asking where Mia's maid of honour or bridesmaids or any female relative might be too.

Carla didn't have anyone but him.

And now Thierry.

And Mia in the short term.

He crossed his fingers and prayed that Thierry would finally give Carla all that she needed...and all that she deserved.

Mia spent two hours with Carla and Dylan, though Dylan rarely spoke now Carla was there. She told herself she was glad. She told herself that she didn't miss his teasing.

Except she did. A little.

Which told her that the way she'd chosen to live her life had a few flaws in it.

Still, even if he had wanted to speak it would have been difficult for him to get a word in, with Carla jumping from topic to topic in a fever of enthusiasm.

She was so different from Carly Smith, the wide-eyed visitor to the park that Mia had taken under her wing. She took in the heightened colour in Carla's cheeks, the way her eyes glittered, how she could barely keep still, and nodded. Love was *exactly* like that and Mia wanted no part of it *ever again*.

Carla spoke at a hundred miles an hour. She cooed about the colour scheme she wanted—pink, of course—and the table decorations she'd seen in a magazine, as well as the cake she'd fallen in love with. She rattled off guest numbers and seating arrangements in one breath and told her about the world-class photographer she was hoping to book in the next. Oh, and then there was the string quartet that was apparently *'divine'*.

She bounced from favours and bouquets to napkins and place settings along with a million other things that Mia hastily jotted down, but the one thing she didn't mention was the bridal party. At one point Mia opened her mouth to ask, but behind his sister's back Dylan surreptitiously shook his head and Mia closed it again.

Maybe Carla hadn't decided on her attendants yet. Mia suspected that the politics surrounding bridesmaid hierarchy could be fraught. Especially for a big society wedding.

Only it wasn't going to be big. It was going to be a very select and exclusive group of fifty guests. Which might mean that Carla didn't want a large bridal party.

Every now and again, though, Carla would falter. She'd glance at her brother and without fail Dylan would step in and smooth whatever wrinkle had brought Carla up short, and then off she would go again.

Beneath Carla's manic excitement Mia sensed a lurking vulnerability, and she couldn't prevent a sense of protectiveness from welling through her. She'd warmed to Carly—Carla—the moment she'd met her. For all her natural warmth and enthusiasm she had seemed a little lost, and it had soothed something inside Mia to chat to her about the programmes Plum Pines ran, to talk to her about the animals and their daily routines.

As a rule, Mia did her best *not* to warm towards people. She did her best not to let them warm towards her either. But to remain coolly professional and aloof with Carla—the way she'd tried to be with Dylan—somehow seemed akin to kicking a puppy.

While many of her work colleagues thought her a cold and unfeeling witch, Mia *didn't* kick puppies. She didn't kick anyone. Except herself—mentally—on a regular basis.

'Can I come back with Thierry tomorrow and go over all this again?'

Why hadn't the groom-to-be been here *today*?

'Yes, of course.'

Hopefully tomorrow Nora would be back to take over and Mia would be safely ensconced on the reserve's eastern boundary, communing with weeds.

Carla glanced at her watch. 'I promised Thierry I'd meet

him for lunch. I have to run.' She turned to her brother. 'Dylan...?' Her voice held a note of warning.

He raised his hands, palms outwards. 'I'll sort everything—I promise. Mia and I will go back to the office and thrash it all out.'

Mia's chest clenched. Thrash what out? She didn't have the authority to thrash *anything* out.

She must have looked crestfallen, because Dylan laughed. 'Buck up, Mia. It'll be fun.' He waggled his eyebrows.

Mia rolled her eyes, but she couldn't crush the anticipation that flitted through her.

'I'll buy you a cup of coffee and a blueberry muffin.'

His grin could melt an ice queen.

Lucky, then, that she was made of sterner stuff than ice.

'You'll do no such thing.' She stowed her notepad in her back pocket as they headed back towards the main concourse. 'Gordon Coulter would be scandalised. All refreshments will be courtesy of Plum Pines.'

During the last two hours they'd moved from the lily pond back to the office, to pore over brochures, and then outside again to a vacant picnic table, where Carla had declared she wanted to drink in the serenity. Now, with many grateful thanks, Carla moved towards the car park while Mia led Dylan to the Pine Plum's café.

He grinned at the cashier, and Mia didn't blame the woman for blinking as if she'd been temporarily blinded.

'We'll have two large cappuccinos and two of those.' He pointed at the cupcakes sitting beneath a large glass dome before Mia had a chance to speak.

'You mean to eat two cupcakes and drink two mugs of coffee?' She tried to keep the acerbity out of her voice.

'No.' He spoke slowly as if to a child. 'One coffee and one cake are yours.'

Mia glanced at the cashier. 'Make that one large cappuccino, one pot of tea and *one* cupcake, thank you. It's to go on Nora's events account.'

Without further ado she led him to a table with an outlook over the duck pond.

'You're not hungry?' he asked.

She was ravenous, but she'd brought her lunch to work, expecting to be stranded on the eastern boundary, and she hated waste. 'I'm not hungry,' she said. It was easier than explaining that in Gordon Coulter's eyes the events account didn't extend to buying her any food. 'Besides, I don't have much of a sweet tooth.'

She frowned, unsure why she'd added that last bit.

For a moment he looked as if he were waging an internal battle with himself, but then he folded his arms on the table and leaned towards her, his eyes dancing. 'Are you telling me, Mia…?'

She swallowed at the way he crooned her name, as if it were the sweetest of sweet things.

'…that you don't like cake?'

He said it with wide eyes, as if the very idea was scandalous. He was teasing her again. She resisted the almost alien urge to tease him back.

'I didn't say I didn't like it. It's just not something I ever find myself craving.'

His mouth kinked at one corner. Mia did her best to look away.

'Now I have to discover what it is you *do* crave.'

How could he make that sound so suggestive?

'Cheesecake? Ice cream?'

She narrowed her eyes. 'Why do I get the feeling you're trying to find something to use as a bribe?'

'Chocolate?'

Oh. He had her there. 'Chocolate is in a class of its own.'

He laughed, and something inside her shifted. *No shifting!* She had to remain on her guard around this man. He'd called her beautiful and something in her world had tilted. She had no intention of letting that happen again.

'You made my sister very happy today. From the bottom of my heart, thank you.'

It was the last thing she'd expected him to say. 'I… I was just doing my job.'

'It was more than that, and we both know it.'

She didn't want it to be more. This was just a job like any other. 'Naturally Carla is excited. I enjoyed discussing her plans with her.'

To her surprise, she realised she was speaking nothing less than the truth.

Their order was set in front of them. When the waitress left Dylan broke off a piece of cupcake, generously topped with frosting, and held it out to her. 'Would you like a taste?'

Unbidden, hunger roared through her. For the briefest of moments she was tempted to open her mouth and let him feed her the morsel. Her throat dried and her stomach churned. On the table, her hands clenched to fists.

She choked out a, 'No, thank you,' before busying herself with her tea.

Why now? Why should a man have such an effect on her *now*? In the last ten months she'd been asked out on dates… the occasional volunteer had tried to flirt with her…but nothing had pierced her armour.

None of them looked like Dylan Fairweather.

True. But was she really so shallow that someone's looks could have such an impact?

When she glanced back up she saw Gordon Coulter, glaring at her from the café's doorway. Had he seen Dylan offer her the bite of cake? *Great. Just great.*

She shuffled her mantel of professionalism back around her. 'Now, you better tell me what it is you promised Carla you'd sort out. It sounded ominous.'

He popped the piece of cake into his mouth and closed his eyes in bliss as he chewed. 'You have no idea what you're missing.'

And she needed to keep it that way.

She tried to stop her gaze lingering on his mouth.

His eyes sprang open, alive with mischief. 'I bet you love honey sandwiches made with the softest of fresh white bread.'

She had to bite her inner lip to stop herself from laughing. 'Honey makes my teeth ache.'

The man was irrepressible, and it occurred to her that it wasn't his startling looks that spoke to her but his childish sense of fun.

'Ha! But I nearly succeeded in making you laugh again.'

She didn't laugh, but she did smile. It was impossible not to.

Mia didn't do fun. Maybe that was a mistake too. Maybe she needed to let a little fun into her life and then someone like Dylan wouldn't rock her foundations so roundly.

He made as if to punch the air in victory. 'You should do that more often. It's not good for you to be so serious all the time.'

His words made her pull back. She knew he was only teasing, but he had no idea what was good for her.

She pulled her notepad from her pocket and flipped it open to a new page. 'Will you *please* tell me what it is you promised Carla you'd take care of?'

He surveyed her as he took a huge bite of cake. She tried not to fidget under that oddly penetrating gaze.

'Don't you ever let your hair down just a little?'

'This is my job. And this—' she gestured around '—is my place of employment. I have a responsibility to my employer to not "let my hair down" on the job.' She tapped her pen against the notepad. 'I think it's probably worth mentioning that you aren't my employer's only wedding account either.'

She spoke gently, but hoped he sensed the thread of steel beneath her words. There also were cages that needed cleaning, animals that needed feeding and logbooks to fill out. They weren't all going to get magically done while Dylan lingered over coffee and cake.

And it didn't matter how much he might temporarily fill her with an insane desire to kick back and take the rest of the day off—that wasn't going to happen.

'Ouch.' He said it with a good-natured grin. 'But you're right. Carla and I have taken up enough of your time for one day. Especially as we'll be back tomorrow.'

He was coming too? She tried to ignore the way her heart hitched.

'Mia, do you know what line of work I'm in?'

Even she, who'd spent most of her adult life living under a rock, knew what Dylan Fairweather did for a living. 'You created and run Fairweather Event Enterprises.' More widely known as Fairweather Events or FWE. Dylan had made his name bringing some of the world's most famous, not to mention *notorious*, rock acts to Australia.

Under his direction, Dylan's company had produced concerts of such spectacular proportions they'd gone down in rock history. His concerts had become a yardstick for all those following.

FWE had been in charge of last year's sensationally successful charity benefit held in Madison Square Garden in New York. He was regularly hired by royalty to oversee national anniversary celebrations, and by celebrities for their private birthday parties and gala events. Dylan Fairweather was a name with a capital N.

'The thing is…' He shuffled towards her, his expression intent now rather than teasing. 'I know that Plum Pines has its own events team, but *I* want to be the person running this particular show.'

Very slowly, she swallowed. 'By *"this particular show"*, I take it you're referring to Carla's wedding?'

He nodded.

Her heart thumped. Nora would be disappointed.

'I want to do this for Carla,' he continued, fully in earnest now. 'The only thing I can give her that's of any worth is my time. You have to understand it's not that I don't trust the Plum Pines staff, it's that I want to give my sister something that'll actually *mean* something to her—something she can cherish forever.'

Mia almost melted on the spot. To have someone who cared about you so much that they'd go to such lengths… That was—

'Mia?'

She started. 'I'm afraid I don't have the kind of clout to authorise an arrangement like that. But I'll present your case to Nora and Mr Coulter. Please be assured they'll do everything they can to accommodate your and Carla's wishes.' She bit her lip. 'They may have some additional questions that they'd like to ask you.' Questions *she* lacked the expertise and foresight to ask.

He immediately slid his business card across the table to her. 'They can contact me at any time.'

She picked it up. It was a simple card on good-quality bond, with embossed lettering in dark blue—a deeper and less interesting shade than his eyes.

He slid another card across the table to her. 'Would you write down your number for me, Mia?'

She dutifully wrote down the Plum Pines office number, along with Nora's work number.

He glanced at it and his lips pursed. 'I was hoping for *your* number.'

Her hand shook as she reached for her tea. 'Why?'

'Because I think you could be an ally. You, I believe, approve of my plan to be Carla's wedding co-ordinator.'

She hesitated. 'I think it's a lovely idea.' Surely it couldn't hurt to admit that much? 'But I think you ought to know that I have very little influence here.'

'I think you're selling yourself short.'

'If you want to speak to me directly, ring the office and ask them to page me.' She couldn't believe she'd told him to do that, but she couldn't find it in herself to regret the offer either.

For a moment she thought he'd press the matter. Instead he stood and held out his hand. 'Until tomorrow, then, Mia.'

She stood too and shook it, eager to be away from him. 'Goodbye, Dylan.'

She didn't tell him that in all likelihood she wouldn't see him tomorrow. Funny how suddenly the eastern boundary didn't seem as exciting a prospect as it had earlier in the day.

She'd barely settled down in the meeting room with the office laptop, to type up her copious notes for Nora, when the receptionist tapped on the glass door.

'Mr Coulter wants to see you, Mia.'

To grill her about how things had gone with the Fairweathers, no doubt. She'd have rather discussed it all with Nora first, but she couldn't very well refuse to speak to him.

Taking a deep breath, she knocked on his door, only entering when he bellowed, 'Come in.'

She left the door ajar. She didn't fully trust Gordon Coulter. 'You wanted to see me?'

'Yes.'

He didn't invite her to sit. The smile he sent her chased ice down her spine.

'It's my very great pleasure to inform you, Ms Maydew, that you're fired. Effective immediately.'

The room spun. Mia's chest cramped. She couldn't lose this job. It was all that she had. Her fingers went cold. She *needed* this job!

'You're terminating my contract? But...*why?*'

Dylan stood on the threshold of Gordon Coulter's office, his head rocking back at the words he heard emerging from the other side of the door.

Gordon Coulter was *firing* Mia?

'Your behaviour with Dylan Fairweather today was scandalous and utterly inappropriate. You're not here to make sexual advances towards our clients. You're here to perform your duties as efficiently and as capably as possible—a duty that's obviously beyond you and your bitch-on-heat morals.'

Darkness threatened the edges of Dylan's vision. Mia hadn't made one inappropriate advance towards him—not one! His hands curled into fists. A pity the same couldn't be said for him towards her. He hadn't been able to resist flirting with her in the café—just a little bit. He hadn't been able to resist making her laugh again.

This was *his* fault. How could he have been so careless as to put her in this position?

Gordon continued to wax lyrical on a list of Mia's imaginary faults and Dylan's insides coiled up, tight and lethal. Gordon Coulter was a pompous ass!

'But even if I was prepared to overlook all that,' Gordon continued, his tone clearly saying that he had no intention of doing so, 'I refuse to disregard the fact that when you entered the emu enclosure you put the safety of a member of the public at risk.'

No way, buddy!

Dylan backed up two steps and then propelled himself forward with a cheery, 'Knock-knock!' before bursting into the office.

Two sets of eyes swung to him. Mia's face was ashen. Guilt plunged through him like a serrated-edge knife.

You're nothing but a trust fund baby without substance or significance.

As true as that might be, it meant that he knew how to act entitled and high-handed. He used that to his advantage now, striding into the room as if he owned it and everything inside it.

'You moved very quickly to bring my proposal to the attention of your superiors, Mia. I can't tell you how much I appreciate it.'

He took a seat across from Gordon, making himself completely at home.

'I hope you realise what a gem you have here, Gordon.'

He pulled Mia down to the seat beside him. How *dared* Gordon leave her standing like some recalcitrant child deserving of punishment and castigation? 'Have you finished telling Gordon about my proposal, Mia?'

'Um…no, not yet.'

She swallowed and he saw how valiantly she hauled her composure back into place. *Atta girl*!

'I'm afraid I haven't had a chance.'

'Oh, before I forget—' Dylan turned back to Gordon '—my sister and I will be returning tomorrow with Thierry. If he approves our plans, and if you accept my proposal, then we'll be booking Plum Pines as Carla and Thierry's wedding venue.'

Dollar signs all but flashed in Gordon's eyes. 'That's splendid news!'

'Carla has requested that Mia be available for tomorrow's meeting. I'm sure that won't be a problem.'

'Well, I—'

'Now to my proposal…' he continued, making it obvious that he took Gordon's agreement for granted. He saw Mia bite her lip, as if to hold back a laugh. The tightness in his chest eased a fraction.

'While I understand that Plum Pines has a talented and capable events team, I want to be completely in charge of Carla's wedding preparations—bringing in my own people, et cetera. I understand this isn't how Plum Pines normally operates, but if I promise to acquire all the necessary licenses and, as a show of gratitude, donate…say…a hundred thousand dollars to the Plum Pines Nature Fund, I was hoping you might make an exception.'

Gordon's fleshy mouth dropped open. He hauled it back into place. 'I'm sure we can find a way to accommodate such a reasonable request from such a generous benefactor.'

Dylan rubbed his hands together. 'Excellent.'

Gordon Coulter was ridiculously transparent. Rumour had it he was planning to run for mayor next year. A donation as sizable as Dylan's would be a real feather in his cap. Dylan just hoped the good people of Newcastle were smart enough not to elect such a small-minded bully to office.

He made a note to donate a large sum to Gordon's opponent's campaign.

'If there's any further way we can assist you, don't hesitate to ask. We're here to provide you with the very best service we can.'

'Well, now that you mention it… Carla would like Mia as her official liaison between FWE and Plum Pines.'

Gordon's face darkened. 'Mia doesn't have the necessary training. We can provide you with a far better level of service than that, and—'

'It's non-negotiable, I'm afraid.' He spoke calmly. 'If there's no Mia there'll be no Fairweather wedding at Plum Pines—and, sadly, no hundred-thousand-dollar donation.'

It was as simple as that, and Gordon could take it or leave it. If he refused to let Mia act as liaison then Dylan would whisk her away from Plum Pines and find a position for her in his own organisation. He was always on the lookout for good people.

In fact, poaching her was a damn fine plan.

Gordon wouldn't pass on it, though. Dylan knew his type too well.

'If you're happy with Mia's limited experience…' he began, in that pompous fashion.

'Supremely so.'

'I'll have to insist that she consult with Nora closely,' he blustered, in an attempt to save face.

'Absolutely.'

Gordon swallowed a few times, his jowls quivering. 'In that case I'll raise no objections.'

Dylan leant back in his chair. 'Excellent.'

Mia leaned forward in hers, her dark gaze skewering Gordon to the spot. 'And our earlier conversation…?'

His mouth opened and closed before he shuffled upright

in his seat. 'In the light of these…new developments, any further action will be suspended—pending your on-the-job performance from here on in.'

Very slowly she leaned back. Dylan silently took in the way her fingers opened and closed around each other. Eventually she nodded. 'Very well.'

Dylan stood. 'I understand you're a busy man, Gordon, so I won't take up any more of your valuable time. Mia…' He turned to her and she shot to her feet. 'I forgot to give you Carla's mobile number. You're going to need it. I'm afraid she'll be leaving you messages day and night.'

'That won't be an issue,' Gordon inserted. 'Mia understands that here at Plum Pines our clients are our priority. She'll be at your sister's beck and call twenty-four-seven.'

Dylan barely restrained himself from reciting the 'Maximum Ordinary Hours of Employment' section of the *New South Wales Industrial Relations Act*. Instead he gestured for Mia to precede him out through the door.

'Lead me to your trusty notepad.'

He closed the door behind them and Mia didn't speak until they were safely ensconced in the meeting room.

She swung to him. 'You did that on purpose, didn't you? You overheard him trying to fire me so you jumped in and saved my job.'

His chest expanded at the way she looked at him—as if he'd ridden in and saved the day.

She pressed a hand to her chest. 'I think I just fell a little bit in love with you.'

She was the strangest mix of seriousness and generosity he'd ever come across. And totally adorable to boot.

He leaned towards her, but she took a step backwards.

'Sorry, I shouldn't have said that. It was a stupid thing to say. I only meant I was grateful—*very* grateful—for you coming to my defence like you did.'

'You're welcome. Gordon is a pompous ass.'

'A pompous ass who has the power to terminate my traineeship whenever he sees fit.'

'He'd need to show good cause in the Industrial Relations Court. Don't you forget that. In fact—' he widened his stance '—why don't you forget Gordon and Plum Pines and come and work for *me*?'

The beginnings of a smile touched her lips. It made his pulse beat that little bit harder.

'I don't believe I have enough...*exuberance* for your line of work, Dylan.'

'I was wrong about that. You're perfect.'

'No, I'm not!' Her voice came out tart. Too tart.

He frowned. 'I meant that your work ethic is perfect. Your customer service skills are impeccable.' That was *all* he'd meant.

She swallowed before gesturing for him to take a seat. 'If you want me working so closely with you and Carla then there's something you need to know about me.'

He sat in the chair at the head of the table. 'I know all I need to know.'

She fixed him with that compelling gaze of hers, but for the life of him he couldn't read her expression. She took the chair immediately to his left, gripping her hands together until her knuckles turned white.

'I'd rather be the one to tell you than for you to hear it from other sources.'

He straightened. What on earth...? 'I'm listening.'

He watched the compulsive bob of her throat as she swallowed. Her hands gripped each other so tightly he was sure she'd cut off the blood supply to her fingers if she weren't careful.

'Ten months ago I was released from jail after serving a three-year prison sentence for committing fraud. I think it's only fair that you know I'm an ex-convict.'

CHAPTER THREE

MIA WAITED WITH a growing sense of dread for Dylan's face to close and for him to turn away.

His open-mouthed shock rang through her like a blow, but his face didn't close. He didn't turn away.

His frown did deepen, though, and she could read the thoughts racing behind the vivid blue of his eyes.

'No,' she said, holding his gaze. 'I wasn't wrongfully convicted, there were no mitigating circumstances.' She swallowed. 'Unless you want to count the fact that I was young and stupid.'

And utterly in thrall to Johnnie Peters. So in love she'd have done anything he'd asked of her. So in love she *had* done anything he'd asked of her.

'You're not going to tell me any more than that?'

Curiosity sharpened his gaze, but it wasn't the kind of avid, voyeuristic curiosity that made her want to crawl under a rock. It held a warmth and sympathy that almost undid her.

Swallowing again, she shook her head. 'It's sordid and unpleasant and it's in the past. According to the justice system, I've paid my debt to society. I won't ever steal again. I'll never break the law again. But I understand that in light of these circumstances my word isn't worth much. I'll completely understand if you'd prefer to deal with Nora rather than with me.'

He didn't say anything.

'You don't need to worry about my job. You've done enough to ensure I won't be fired…at least, not this week.' She'd aimed for levity, but it fell flat.

He lifted his chin. 'I meant what I said—come and work for me.'

She realised now what she'd known on a subconscious level after only ten minutes in his company—Dylan Fairweather was a good man.

'I appreciate the offer, I really do, but besides the fact that you don't know me—'

'I know you have a good work ethic. If the way you've treated Carla is anything to go by, where clients are concerned nothing is too much trouble for you. They're valuable assets in an employee.'

'According to Gordon I have a problem with authority.'

He grinned, and leaned in so close she could smell the nutmeg warmth of his skin. 'That's something we have in common, then.'

How was it possible for him to make her laugh when they were having such a serious conversation? She sobered, recalling her earlier impulsive, *I think I just fell a little bit in love with you.* She should never have said it. Instinct warned her that Dylan could wreak havoc on her heart if she let him.

She couldn't let him. She wasn't giving *any* man that kind of power over her again.

She pulled in a breath. 'I was fortunate to be awarded this traineeship. The opportunity was given to me in good faith and I feel honour-bound to make the most of it.'

'Admirable.'

It wasn't admirable at all. She needed a job—a way to earn a living. For the two-year tenure of her traineeship she'd be in paid employment. Maybe at the end of that time she'd have proved herself worthy and someone would take a chance on employing her. She needed a way to support herself. After what she'd done she couldn't ask the welfare system to support her.

'Do you have a passion for conservation?'

'Conservation is an important issue.'

'That's not the same thing,' he pointed out.

Passion was dangerous. She'd done all she could to excise it from her life. Besides, busying herself with weed extermination programmes, soil erosion projects, and koala breeding strategies—plants, dirt and animals—meant she had minimal contact with people.

And as far as she was concerned that was a *very* good thing.

'Here.' He pulled a chocolate bar from his pocket. 'This is the real reason I came back to the office.'

Frowning, she took it, careful not to touch him as she did so.

'You said chocolate belonged in a class of its own and...'

He shrugged, looking a little bit embarrassed, and something inside her started to melt.

No melting!

'I wanted to thank you for your patience with both Carla and me today.'

'It's—'

'I know—it's your job, Mia.'

Dear Lord, the way he said her name...

'But good work should always be acknowledged. And...' An irrepressible smile gathered at the corner of his mouth. 'I fear more of the same will be asked of you tomorrow.'

It took a moment for his words to sink in. 'You mean...?'

'I mean we want *you*, Mia. Not Nora. I want everything associated with this wedding to be a joy for Carla. She likes you. And that's rarer than you might think.' He suddenly frowned. 'How much will taking charge of this affect your traineeship? Will I be creating a problem for you there?'

He was giving her an out. If she wanted one. *If...*

She pulled in a breath. 'The wedding is nine months away, right?'

He nodded.

Being Carla's liaison wouldn't be a full-time job. Very slowly she nodded too. 'That leaves me plenty of time to continue with my fieldwork and studies.'

If it weren't for Dylan she wouldn't have a job right now *or* a chance to finish her traineeship. She owed him. *Big-time.* She made a resolution then and there to do all she could to make Carla's wedding a spectacular success.

Her gaze rested on the chocolate bar he'd handed to her earlier. She suddenly realised how she could tacitly thank him right now. Without giving herself time to think, she ripped off the wrapper and bit into it.

'I'm ravenous. And this is *so* good.'

As she'd known he would, he grinned in delight that his gift had given her pleasure. She closed her eyes to savour the soft milky creaminess, and when she opened them again she found his gaze fastened on her lips, the blue of his eyes deepening and darkening, and her stomach pitched.

She set the chocolate to the table and wiped damp palms down her trousers. 'I... This is probably a stupid thing to raise...'

He folded his arms. 'Out with it.'

'I don't believe you have any interest in me beyond that of any employer, but after what Gordon just accused me of...'

She couldn't meet his eyes. The thing was, Gordon had recognised what she'd so desperately wanted to keep hidden—that she found Dylan attractive. *Very* attractive. He'd woken something inside her that she desperately wanted to put back to sleep.

'I just want to make it clear that I'm not in the market for a relationship. *Any* kind of relationship—hot and heavy or fun and flirty.'

She read derision in his eyes. But before she could dissolve into a puddle of embarrassment at his feet she realised the derision was aimed at himself—not at her.

'No relationships? Noted.' He rolled his shoulders. 'Mia, I have a tendency to flirt—it's a result of the circles I move in—but it doesn't mean anything. It's just supposed to be a bit of harmless fun. My clients like to feel important and, as *they* are important to me, I like to make them feel valued. I plan celebrations, parties, and it's my job to make the entire process as enjoyable as possible. So charm and a sense of fun have become second nature to me. If I've given you the wrong impression...'

'Oh, no, you haven't!'

'For what it's worth, I'm not in the market for a relationship at the moment either.'

She glanced up.

Why not?

That's no concern of yours.

Humour flitted through his eyes. 'But what about friendship? Do you have anything against that?'

That made her smile. People like Dylan didn't become friends with people like her. Once the wedding was over she'd never see him again.

'I have nothing whatsoever against friendship.' She'd sworn never again to steal or cheat. A little white lie, though, didn't count. Did it...?

Thierry Geroux, Carla's fiancé, was as dark and scowling as Carla and Dylan were golden and gregarious. Mia couldn't help but wonder what on earth Carla saw in him.

She pushed that thought away. It was none of her business.

As if he sensed the direction of her thoughts, Thierry turned his scowl on her. She wanted to tell him not to bother—that his scowls didn't frighten *her*...she'd been scowled at by professionals. She didn't, of course. She just sent him one of the bland smiles she'd become so adept at.

'Do you have any questions, Mr Geroux?' He'd barely spoken two words in the last hour.

'No.'

'None?' Dylan double-checked, a frown creasing his brow.

'Stop bouncing,' Thierry said in irritation to Carla, who

clung to his arm, shifting her weight from one leg to the other.

'But, Thierry, it's so *exciting*!'

Nevertheless she stopped bouncing.

Thierry turned to Dylan. 'Carla is to have the wedding she wants. As you're the events expert, I'm sure you have that under control.'

He ignored Mia completely. Which suited Mia just fine.

Dylan turned back to Mia. 'There could be quite a gap between the end of the wedding ceremony and the start of the reception, while Carla and Thierry have photographs taken.'

Mia nodded. 'It;s often the case. With it being late spring there'll still be plenty of light left. I can organise a tour of the wildlife exhibits for those who are interested.'

'Oh!' Carla jumped up and down. 'Could we do that now?'

'Absolutely.'

The exhibits—a system of aviaries and enclosures—were sympathetically set into the natural landscape. A wooden walkway meandered through the arrangement at mid-tree height. This meant visitors could view many of the birds at eye level, practically commune with the rock wallabies sunning themselves on their craggy hillside, and look down on the wombats, echidnas and goannas in their pens.

At the heart of the wildlife walk—and the jewel in its crown—was the koala house. Set up like an enormous tree house, the wooden structure was covered on three sides to weatherproof it for visitors, with an arena opening out below full of native flora and an artfully designed pond.

The entire complex was enclosed in a huge aviary. A visitor could glance up into the trees to view the variety of colourful parrots, or along the rafters of the tree house to see the napping tawny frogmouths. Below were a myriad of walking birds, along with the occasional wallaby and echidna. But at eye-level were the koalas on their specially designed poles, where fresh eucalyptus leaves were placed daily. No wire or special glass separated man from beast—only a wooden railing and a ten-foot drop into the enclosure below.

'I *love* this place,' Carla breathed as they entered.

'This is really something,' Dylan murmured in Mia's ear.

His breath fanned the hair at her temples and awareness skidded up her spine. 'It's a special place,' she agreed, moving away—needing to put some distance between them.

When they'd looked their fill, she led them back outside to a series of small nocturnal houses—the first of which was the snake house.

Carla gave a shudder. 'No matter how much I try, I don't like snakes.'

They didn't bother Mia, but she nodded. 'We don't have to linger. We can move straight on to the amphibian house and then the possum house.'

'C'mon, Thierry.'

Carla tugged on his arm, evidently eager to leave, but he disengaged her hand. 'You go ahead. I find snakes fascinating.'

Finally the man showed some interest—*hallelujah!*

Thierry glanced at her. 'Mia might be kind enough to stay behind with me and answer some questions?'

The snakes might not bother her, but Mia loathed the caged darkness of the nocturnal houses, hating the way they made her feel trapped. She didn't betray any of that by so much of a flicker of her eyelids, though.

'I'd be happy to answer any questions.'

Dylan caught her eye and gestured that he and Carla would move on, and she nodded to let him know that she and Thierry would catch up.

She moved to stand beside Thierry, nodding at the slender green snake with the bright yellow throat that he currently surveyed. 'That's a tree snake. It's—'

'I can read.'

She sucked in a breath. Was he being deliberately rude?

She lifted her chin. He might be hard work, but she was used to hard work.

'They're very common,' she continued, 'but rarely seen as they're so shy. They seldom bite. Their main form of defence is to give off a rather dreadful odour when threatened.'

Mia was convinced there was a metaphor for life trapped in there somewhere.

'*You* give off a bad smell too.'

Thierry moved so quickly that before she knew what he was doing he had her trapped between the wall and a glass display unit—the olive python on the other side didn't stir.

'Dylan told us about your background—that you're nothing but a common little thief with a criminal record.'

The sudden sense of confinement had her heart leaping into her throat before surging back into her chest to thump off the walls of her ribs.

'When I was in jail—' with a supreme effort she kept her voice utterly devoid of emotion '—I learned a lot about self-defence and how to hurt someone. If you don't take two steps back within the next three seconds you're going to find yourself on your back in a screaming mess of pain.'

He waited the full three seconds, but he did move away. Mia tried to stop her shoulders from sagging as she dragged a grateful breath into her lungs.

He stabbed a finger at her. 'I don't like you.'

And that should matter to me because...? She bit the words back. She'd had a lot of practice at swallowing sarcastic rejoinders. She'd made it a policy long ago not to inflame a situation if she could help it.

'Carla and Dylan are too trusting by half—but you won't find *me* so gullible.'

Giving a person the benefit of the doubt did *not* make Dylan gullible.

'You're not a fit person for Carla to know. You stay away from her, you hear? If you don't I'll cause trouble for you... and that's a promise.'

'Is everything okay here?'

A strip of sunlight slashed through the darkness as Dylan came back through the doors. The doors were merely thick flaps of overlapping black rubber that kept the sun out. A few threads of light backlit him, haloing his head and shading his face. Mia didn't need to see his face to sense the tension rippling through him.

Without another word Thierry snapped away and moved through the rubber panels, his footsteps loud on the wooden walkway as he strode off.

'Are you okay?'

Dylan's concern, absurdly, made her want to cry in a way that Thierry's threats hadn't.

'Yes, of course.' She turned and gestured to the snakes. 'Just so you know: a reptile encounter can be arranged for the wedding guests too, if anyone's interested. Though it has to be said it's not to everyone's taste.'

Dylan took Mia's arm and led her back out into the sunshine, wincing at her pallor.

Her colour started to return after a few deep breaths and he found the rapid beat of his heart slowed in direct proportion.

'I heard the last part of what Thierry said to you.'

He hadn't liked the way Thierry had asked Mia to stay behind. It was why he'd doubled back—to make sure everything was okay.

'It's not the first time someone has taken exception to my past, Dylan, and I expect it won't be the last.'

Her revelation yesterday had shocked him— *prison!*—but he'd have had to be blind not to see how much she regretted that part of her life. He'd sensed her sincerity in wanting to create a new, honest life for herself. She'd paid dearly for whatever mistakes lay in her past. As far as he was concerned she should be allowed to get on with things in peace.

Thierry's threat, the utter contempt in his voice...

Dylan's hands clenched. It had been a long time since he'd wanted to knock someone to the ground. He'd wanted to deck Thierry, though. He'd wanted to beat the man black and blue.

He dragged a hand down his face. It had only been the thought of who'd pay for his actions—Mia—that had stopped him.

You didn't even think of Carla!

Mia stared up at him, her gaze steady. 'Don't blame Thierry. He only has Carla's welfare in mind.'

'It doesn't excuse his behaviour.' A scowl scuffed through him. 'The man's a bully and a jerk. What the hell does Carla see in him?'

She gestured that they should continue along the path towards the amphibian house. 'Don't you know?'

He didn't have a single clue.

'Haven't the two of you talked about him?'

Not really. But to say as much would only reveal what a poor excuse for a brother he'd been to Carla these last twelve months.

He glanced across at Mia and found that she'd paled again, but before he could ask her if she was okay she'd plunged into the darkness of the amphibian house. Was she worried about running into Thierry again?

He plunged right in after her.

'Do you want to linger?'

He couldn't have said how he knew, but he sensed the tension coiling through her. 'No.'

She led them back outside and gulped in a couple of breaths. She stilled when she realised how closely he watched her.

He reached out to stop her from moving on. 'What's wrong?'

She glanced away. 'What makes you think anything's wrong?'

When she turned back, he just shrugged.

Her shoulders sagged. 'I'd rather nobody else knew this.'

Silently, he crossed his heart.

She looked away again. 'I don't like the nocturnal houses. They make me feel claustrophobic and closed in.

They were like being in jail!

He had to stiffen his legs to stop himself from pitching over.

'I'm fine out here on the walkways, where we're above or beside the enclosures and aviaries, but the nocturnal houses are necessarily dark...and warm. The air feels too close.'

She finished with a deprecating little shrug that broke his heart a little bit.

In the next moment he was gripped with an avid need to know everything about her—were her parents still alive? How had they treated her when she was a child? What made her happy? What did she really want from life? What frightened her right down to her bones? What did she do in her spare time? What made her purr?

That last thought snapped him back. He had no right to ask such questions. He shouldn't even be considering them. What he should be doing was working out if Carla was about to make the biggest mistake of her life. *That* was what he should be focussed on.

'What about when you're down below?' he found himself asking anyway. 'When you have to go into the cages to clean them out...to feed the animals?'

He saw the answer in her eyes before she drew that damn veil down over them again.

'It's okay. It's just another part of the job.'

Liar. He didn't call her on it. It was none of his business. But it begged the question—why was Mia working in a place like this when enclosed spaces all but made her hyperventilate?

They found Carla and Thierry waiting for them beside the kangaroo enclosure.

The moment she saw Mia, Carla grabbed her arm. 'I want to become a volunteer!'

Mia smiled as if she couldn't help it 'Volunteers are always welcome at Plum Pines.'

Her tone held no awkwardness and Dylan's shoulders unhitched a couple of notches. Thierry's strictures hadn't constrained the warmth she showed to Carla, and he gave silent thanks for it.

Thierry pulled Mia back to his side, gently but inexorably. 'Stop manhandling the staff, Carla.'

Dylan lifted himself up to his full height. 'That's an insufferably snobbish thing to say, Thierry.'

Carla's face fell and he immediately regretted uttering the words within her earshot.

Thierry glared back at him. '*You* might be happy consorting with criminals, Dylan, but you'll have to excuse me for being less enthused.'

'Ex.' Mia's voice cut through the tension, forcing all eyes to turn to her. 'I'm an *ex*-criminal, Mr Geroux. Naturally, I don't expect you to trust me, but you can rest assured that if my employers have no qualms about either my conduct or my ability to perform the tasks required of me, then you need have no worries on that head either.'

'We *don't* have qualms!' Carla jumped in, staring at Thierry as if a simple glare would force him to agree with her.

Thierry merely shrugged. 'Is volunteering such a good idea? You could catch something…get bitten…and didn't you notice the frightful stench coming from the possums?'

'Oh, I hadn't thought about the practicalities…'

She glanced at Mia uncertainly and Dylan wanted to throw his head back and howl.

'You'd need to be up to date with your tetanus shots. All the information is on the Plum Pines website, and I can give you some brochures if you like. You can think about it for a bit, and call the volunteer co-ordinator if you have any questions.'

Thierry scowled at her, but she met his gaze calmly. 'Maybe it's something the two of you could do together.'

Carla clapped her hands, evidently delighted with the idea.

Thierry glanced at his watch with an abrupt, 'We have to go.' He said goodbye to Dylan, ignoring Mia completely, before leading Carla away.

'An absolute charmer,' Dylan muttered under his breath.

Mia had to have heard him, but she didn't say anything, turning instead to a kangaroo waiting on the other side of the fence and feeding it some titbit she'd fished from her pocket. He glanced back at Carla and a sickening cramp stretched through his stomach—along with a growing sense of foreboding.

Mia nudged him, and then held out a handful of what looked like puffed wheat. 'Would you like to feed the kangaroo?'

With a sense of wonder, he took it and fed the kangaroo. He even managed to run his fingers through the fur of the kangaroo's neck. The tightness in him eased.

'Do you have anything pressing you need to attend to in the next couple of hours?'

She shook her head. 'Nora has instructed me to give you all the time and assistance you need. Later this afternoon, if I'm free, she's going to run through some things that I probably need to know—help me create a checklist.'

'Will you meet me at the lily pond in fifteen minutes?'

She blinked, but nodded without hesitation. 'Yes, of course.'

Mia was sitting at the picnic table waiting for him—her notepad at the ready—when he arrived with his bag of goodies.

If he hadn't been so worried about Carla's situation he'd

have laughed at the look on her face when he pulled forth sandwiches, chocolate bars and sodas.

'This is a working lunch, Mia, not some dastardly plot to seduce you.'

Pink flushed her cheeks. 'I never considered anything else for a moment.'

To be fair, she probably hadn't. She'd made it clear where she stood yesterday. When he'd gone back over her words it had struck him that she really *hadn't* thought him interested in her. She'd just been setting boundaries. And if that boundary-setting hadn't been for his benefit, then it had to have been for hers. Which was interesting.

He took the seat beside her rather than the one opposite.

Why was Mia so determined to remain aloof?

He didn't want her aloof.

He wanted her help.

He took her notepad and pen and put them in his pocket. 'You won't need those.' He pushed the stack of sandwiches, a can of soda and a couple of chocolate bars towards her. 'Eat up while I talk.'

She fixed him with those moss-green eyes, but after a moment gave a shrug and reached for the topmost sandwich. She didn't even check to see what it was.

He gestured to the stack. 'I didn't know what you'd like so I got a variety.' He'd grabbed enough to feed a small army, but he'd wanted to make sure he bought something she liked.

She shrugged again. 'I'm not fussy. I'll eat pretty much anything.'

He had a sudden vision of her in prison, eating prison food, and promptly lost his appetite.'

'Dylan?'

He snapped his attention back. 'Sorry, I'm a bit distracted.'

She bit into her sandwich and chewed, simply waiting for him to speak. It occurred to him that if he wanted her help he was going to have to be honest with her.

A weight pressed down on him. Yesterday afternoon she'd looked at him with such gratitude and admiration—as if he were a superhero. Nobody had ever looked at him like that. He didn't want to lose it so quickly.

Not even for Carla's sake?

He straightened. He'd do anything for Carla.

He opened his can of soft drink and took a long swallow before setting it back down. 'I'm ashamed to admit this, but over the last twelve months I've neglected Carla shamefully. She and Thierry have only been dating six months, and the news of their engagement came as a shock. This will probably sound ridiculously big brotherly, but... I'm worried she's making a mistake.'

Mia stared at him for a moment. 'You and Carla seem very close.'

'We are.'

'So why haven't you spent much time together recently?'

How much of the truth did he have to tell her?

He scrubbed a hand through his hair. 'There's an older family member who I have...difficulties with. It's impossible to avoid him when I'm in Australia, and I've wanted to avoid a falling out, so...'

'So you've spent a lot of time overseas instead?'

'Rather than putting up with said family member, I flitted off to organise parties. There was a Turkish sultan's sixtieth birthday party, and then a twenty-fifth wedding anniversary celebration for a couple of members of the British aristocracy. I did some corporate work on the Italian Grand Prix. Oh, and there was a red carpet film premiere that I did just for fun.'

She blinked, as if he'd just spoken in a foreign language. In some ways he supposed he had.

'So there you have it—I'm a coward.'

He lifted his arms and let them drop, waiting for her eyes to darken with scorn. She just stared back at him and waited for him to continue, her gaze not wavering.

He swallowed. 'I came home for Carla's birthday...and for two days over Christmas.' It hadn't been enough! 'That's when she announced her engagement. That's when I realised I'd spent too long away.'

But Carla had finally seemed so settled...so happy. She'd refused to come and work for FWE, preferring to focus on her charity work. Nothing had rung alarm bells for him... until he'd met Thierry.

Mia didn't say anything, but he could tell from her eyes how intently she listened.

'When I heard what he said to you in the reptile house I wanted to knock him to the ground.'

She halted mid-chew, before swallowing. 'I'm very glad you didn't.'

It had only been the thought that Gordon would some-how bring the blame back to her and she'd lose her job that had stilled his hand.

'What he said to you...' His hand clenched and un-clenched convulsively around his can of drink. 'I'm sorry you were put into a position where you were forced to lis-ten to that.'

'It's not your responsibility to apologise on behalf of other people, Dylan.'

Maybe not, but it *felt* like his fault. If he'd taken the time to get to know Thierry better before now...

She reached out and placed a sandwich in front of him. 'And you need to remember that just because he dislikes *me*, and my background, it doesn't necessarily make him a bad person.'

Dylan was far from sure about that.

'Even if I didn't have a criminal record, there's no law that says Thierry has to *like* me.'

'Mia, it's not the fact that he doesn't like you or even that he was rude to you that worries me. What disturbs me is the fact that he threatened you.'

'I can take care of myself.'

She said the words quietly and he didn't doubt her. He wished she didn't *have* to take care of herself. He wished she was surrounded by an army of people who'd take care of her. He sensed that wasn't the case, and suddenly he wanted to buy her a hundred chocolate bars… But what good would that do?

No substance, Dylan Fairweather. You don't have an ounce of substance.

The words roared through him. He pulled air in through his nose and let it out through his mouth—once, twice.

'I have less confidence,' he said finally, 'in Carla's ability to take care of herself.' He met Mia's dark-eyed gaze. 'What if he talks to *her* the way he spoke to you? What if he threatens *her* in the same way he threatened you?'

CHAPTER FOUR

DYLAN COULDN'T KNOW it, but each word raised a welt on Mia's soul. The thought of a woman as lovely as Carla, as open and kind as she was, being controlled and manipulated, possibly even abused, by a man claiming to love her...

It made her stomach burn acid.

It made her want to run away at a hundred miles an hour in the other direction.

She recalled how Thierry had trapped her against the wall in the reptile house and her temples started to throb.

She set her sandwich down before she mangled it. 'Have you seen anything to give you cause for concern before now?'

Those laughing lips of his, his shoulders, and even the laughter lines fanning out from his eyes—all drooped. Her heart burned for him. She wanted to reach out and cover his hand, to offer him whatever comfort she could.

Don't be an idiot.

Dylan might be all golden flirtatious charm, but it didn't mean he'd want someone like *her* touching him. She chafed her left forearm, digging her fingers into the muscle to try and loosen the tension that coiled her tight. She wasn't qualified to offer advice about family or relationships, but even *she* could see what he needed to do.

'Can't...?' She swallowed to counter a suddenly dry throat. 'Can't you talk to Carla and share your concerns?'

'And say what? *Carla, I think the man you're about to marry is a complete and utter jerk?*' He gave a harsh laugh. 'She'd translate that as me forcing her to choose between her brother and her fiancé.'

From the look on his face, it was evident he didn't think she'd choose him. She thought back to the way Carla had clung to Thierry's arm and realised Dylan might have a point.

'How about something a little less confrontational?' She reached for a can of soda, needing something to do with her hands. 'Something like... *Carla, Thierry strikes me as a bit moody. Are you sure he treats you well?*'

He gave a frustrated shake of his head. 'She'd still read it as me criticising her choice. I'd have to go to great lengths to make it as clear as possible that I'm not making her choose between me and Thierry, but the fact of the matter is—regardless of what I discover—I have no power to stop this wedding unless it's what Carla wants. And if she *does* marry him and he *is* cruel to her... I want her to feel she's able to turn to me without feeling constrained because I warned her off him.'

His logic made sense, in a roundabout way, but it still left her feeling uneasy. 'You know, you don't have a lot to go on, here. One incident isn't necessarily indicative of the man. Perhaps you need to make a concerted effort to get to know him better.'

'I mean to. I'm already on it.' Her surprise must have shown, because he added. 'It doesn't take fifteen minutes to buy a few sandwiches, Mia. I made a couple of phone calls before meeting you here.'

She frowned, not really knowing what that meant. 'Did you find out anything?'

'Not yet.'

And then she realised exactly what he'd done. 'You hired a private investigator?'

'Yep.'

'Don't you think that's a little extreme?'

'Not when my sister's happiness and perhaps her physical well-being is at stake.'

She recalled Thierry's latent physical threat to her and thought Dylan might have a point. Still…

'I want to ask for your assistance, Mia.'

'Mine?' she squeaked. What on earth did he think *she* could do?

'I want you to befriend Carla. She might confide in you—especially as Thierry has made it clear that he doesn't like you.'

Had he gone mad? 'Dylan, I can be as friendly towards Carla as it's possible to be.' She'd already resolved to do so. 'But when we get right down to it I'm just one of the many people helping to organise her wedding. We don't exactly move in the same social circles.'

'I've thought about that too. And I've come up with a solution.'

She had a premonition that she wasn't going to like what came next.

He leaned towards her. 'If Carla thought that we were dating—'

'No!' She shot so far away from him she was in danger of falling off the bench.

He continued to survey her, seeming not put off in the least by her vehemence. He unwrapped a chocolate bar and bit into it. 'Why not?'

She wanted to tell him to eat a sandwich first—put something proper into his stomach—but it wasn't her place…and it was utterly beside the point.

'Because I don't date!'

'It wouldn't be *real* dating,' he said patiently. 'It'd be pretend dating.'

She slapped a hand to her chest. 'I work hard to keep a low profile. I don't need my past coming back and biting me more often than it already does. I have a plan for my life,

Dylan—to finish my field officer training and find work in a national park. Somewhere rural—' *remote* '—and quiet, where I can train towards becoming a ranger. All I want is a quiet life so I can live peacefully and stay out of trouble. Dating you *won't* help me achieve that. You live your life up among the stars. You're high-profile.' She pointed to herself. 'Low-profile. Can you see how that's not going to work?'

He tapped a finger against his mouth. 'It's a valid point.'

He leaned towards her, his lips pressed into a firm, persuasive line. It took an effort not to let her attention become distracted by those lips.

'What if I promise to keep your name out of the papers?'

'How? Australia's golden-boy bachelor slumming it with an ex-jailbird? *That* story's too juicy to keep under wraps.'

Heaven only knew what Gordon Coulter would do with a headline like that.

'I've learned over the years how to be *very* discreet. I swear to you that nobody will suspect a thing.'

'Will Thierry be discreet too?' she asked, unable to hide the scorn threading her voice as she recalled his threat to make trouble for her.

'You leave Thierry to me.'

With pleasure.

Dylan pushed his shoulders back, a steely light gleaming in his eyes, and she had to swallow. The golden charmer had gone—had been replaced by someone bigger, harder...and far more intimidating. Beneath his laughing, charismatic allure, she sensed that Dylan had a warrior's heart.

His nostrils flared. 'I'll make sure he doesn't touch you.'

She couldn't have said why, but she believed him—implicitly. Her heart started to thud too hard, too fast. 'Dylan, surely you'd be better off concocting this kind of scheme with one of Carla's friends? They'd—'

'She doesn't have any. Not close. Not any more.'

Why ever not?

His face turned to stone, but his eyes flashed fire. 'Two years ago Carla's boyfriend ran off with her best friend.'

Mia closed her eyes.

'Carla went into a deep depression and pushed all her friends away. She's never been the sort of person to have a lot of close friends—a large social circle, perhaps, but only one or two people she'd consider close—and…'

'And it was all a mess after such a betrayal,' she finished for him, reading it in his face and wanting to spare him the necessity of having to say it out loud. 'Loyalties were divided and some fences never mended.'

He nodded.

She leapt up, needing to work off the agitation coursing through her. 'Dylan, I…'

'What?'

She swung back to him. 'I don't know how we can pull off something like that—pretending to date—convincingly.'

She sat again, feeling like a goose for striding around and revealing her agitation. When she glanced across at him the expression in his eyes made her stomach flip-flop. In one smooth motion he slid across until they were almost touching. He smelt fresh and clean, like sun-warmed cotton sheets, and her every sense went on high alert.

He touched the backs of his fingers to her cheek and she sucked in a breath, shocked at her need to lean into the contact. Oh, this was madness!

'Dylan, I—'

His thumb pressed against her mouth, halting her words. Then he traced the line of her bottom lip and a pulse thumped to life inside her. She couldn't stop her lip from softening beneath his touch, or her mouth from parting ever so slightly so she could draw the scent of him into her lungs.

'I don't think you realise how lovely you are.'

Somewhere nearby a peacock honked. Something splashed in the lily pond. But all Mia could focus on was the man in front of her, staring down at her as if…as if she were a cream bun he'd like to devour…slowly and deliciously.

It shocked her to realise that in that moment she wanted nothing more than to *be* a cream bun.

Dangerous.

The word whispered through her. Some part of her mind registered it, but she was utterly incapable of moving away and breaking the spell Dylan had woven around them.

'Sweet and lovely Mia.'

The low, warm promise in his voice made her breath catch.

'I think we're going to have exactly the opposite problem. I think if we're not careful we could be in danger of being *too* convincing…we could be in danger of convincing ourselves that a lie should become the truth.'

A fire fanned through her. Yesterday, when he'd flirted with her, hadn't it just been out of habit? Had he meant it? He found her attractive?

'Dylan…' His name whispered from her. She didn't mean it to.

His eyes darkened at whatever he saw in her face. 'I dreamed of you last night.'

Dangerous.

The word whispered through her again.

But it didn't feel dangerous. It felt *right* to be whispering secrets to each other.

His thumb swept along the fullness of her bottom lip again, pulling against it to explore the damp moistness inside, sensitising it almost beyond bearing. Unable to help herself, she flicked out her tongue to taste him.

'Mia…' He groaned out her name as if it came from some deep, hidden place.

His head moved towards her, his lips aiming to replace his thumb, and her soul suddenly soared.

Dangerous.

Dangerous and glorious. This man had mesmerised her from the moment she'd first laid eyes on him and—

Mesmerised...?

Dangerous!

With a half-sob Mia fisted her hands in his shirt, but didn't have the strength to push him away. She dropped her chin, ensuring that his kiss landed on her brow instead of her lips.

She felt rather than heard him sigh.

After three hard beats of her heart she let him go. In another two he slid back along the bench away from her.

'As I said, I don't think being convincing will be a problem. However much you might deny it, something burns between us—something that could be so much more than a spark if we'd let it.'

It would be foolish to deny it now.

'Why do you have a no-dating rule?' he asked.

His words pulled her back. With an effort, she found her voice. 'It keeps me out of trouble.'

He remained silent, as if waiting for more, but Mia refused to add anything else.

'Maybe one day you'll share your reasoning with me, but until then I fully mean to respect your rules, Mia.'

He did? She finally glanced up at him.

The faintest of smiles touched his lips. 'And, unlike you, I'm more than happy to share my reasons. One—' he held up a finger '—if I don't respect your no-dating rule I suspect I have no hope of winning your co-operation where Carla's concerned.'

Self-interest? At least that was honest.

He held up a second finger. 'And, two, it seems to me you already have enough people in your life who don't respect your wishes. I don't mean to become one of their number.'

Despite her best efforts, some of the ice around her heart cracked.

He stared at her for a long moment, his mouth turning

grim. 'I fancied myself in love once, but when things got tough the girl in question couldn't hack it. She left. Next time I fall in love it'll be with a woman who can cope with the rough as well as the smooth.'

His nostrils flared, his eyes darkening, and Mia wondered if he'd gone back to that time when the girl in question had broken his heart. She wanted to reach out and touch his hand, pull him back to the present.

She dragged her hands into her lap. 'I'm sorry, Dylan.'

He shook himself. 'It's true that I'm attracted to you, but you've just pointed out how very differently we want to live our lives—high-profile, low-profile. In the real world, that continual push and pull would make us miserable.'

Mia had to look away, but she nodded to let him know that she agreed. It didn't stop her heart from shrivelling to the size of a gum nut.

'Your no-dating rule obviously rules out a fling?'

'It does.' Anything else would be a disaster.

'So these are our ground rules. With those firmly in place we shouldn't have any misunderstandings or false hopes, right? We just need to remember the reasons why we're not dating at the moment, why we're not looking for a relationship, and that'll keep us safe.'

She guessed so.

He drummed his fingers on the picnic table. 'It occurs to me that I haven't given you much incentive to help me out. I'm a selfish brute.'

His consideration for Carla proved that was a lie.

'I've no intention of taking advantage of you. I'm fully prepared to pay you for your time.'

She flinched at his words, throwing an arm up to ward them off. 'I don't want your *money*, Dylan.'

What kind of person did he think she was?

A thief!

She dragged in a breath. 'I went to jail for fraud. Do you think I'd accept money under dubious circumstances again?'

He swore at whatever he saw in her face. 'I'm sorry—that was incredibly insensitive. I didn't mean I thought you could be bought. I just meant it's perfectly reasonable for you to be financially compensated for your time.'

'No.'

'It doesn't have to be dubious. I'd have a contract drawn up so there wasn't a hint of illegality about it.'

His earnestness made the earlier sting fade, but… 'Tell that to the judge.'

He looked stricken for a moment—until he realised she was joking.

'No money changes hands between us,' she said.

He looked as if he wanted to keep arguing with her, but finally he nodded. 'Okay.'

She let out a pent-up breath.

'So, Mia, what I need to know is…what do *you* want? You help me. I help you.'

He'd already saved her job. She hated to admit it, but that made her beholden to him. She rubbed her forehead. Besides, if Carla was in danger of being controlled, dominated, bullied… She swallowed, remembering Johnnie Peters and all he'd convinced her to do. She remembered how she'd sold her soul to a man who'd used her for his own ends and then thrown her away. If Carla were in danger, this would be a way for Mia to start making amends—finding redemption—for the mistakes of the past.

The thought made her stomach churn. She didn't want to do this.

What? You think redemption is easy? You think it's supposed to be a picnic? It should be hard. You should suffer.

She brushed a hand across her eyes, utterly weary with herself.

'What do you want, Mia.'

She wanted to keep her job. Yesterday she'd have trusted him with that piece of information. Today— She glanced across at him. Today she wasn't convinced that he wouldn't use it against her as a weapon to force her co-operation.

Who are you kidding? You already know you're going to help him. No force necessary.

But it would be unwise of her to forget that beneath the smiling charm Dylan had a warrior's heart. And warriors could be utterly ruthless.

She forced her mind off Dylan and to her own situation. He'd ensured her job was safe for the moment...and for the next nine months until Carla's wedding took place. She'd have less than six months left on her traineeship then. Surely she could avoid Gordon's notice in that time? Hopefully he'd be busy with council elections.

If Carla's wedding takes place.

'There has to be something you want,' Dylan persisted, pushing a chocolate bar across to her.

What *did* she want? One thing came immediately to mind.

She picked up the bar of chocolate and twirled it around. 'Carla's wedding is going to be a big deal, right?'

'A huge deal. If it goes ahead.'

She glanced at him. 'If Thierry does turn out to be your worst nightmare, but Carla still insists on marrying him, will you still go ahead and give her the wedding she's always dreamed of?'

A muscle worked in his jaw. 'Yes.'

She couldn't explain why, but that eased some of the tightness in her shoulders. She stared down at the chocolate bar. 'So—considering this low profile of mine—when you and your people start distributing press releases and giving media interviews about the wedding, I'd like you to give the credit to Plum Pines and Nora and FWE without mentioning my name at all.'

His brows drew down over his eyes. 'But that's unfair! Credit should go where it's due. Being associated with Carla's wedding could open doors for you.'

Or it could bring her past and the scandal to the front pages of the gossip rags. 'You asked me what I wanted. I'm simply telling you.'

He swung back to scowl at the lily pond. 'I don't like it. It goes against the grain. But if it's what you really want, then consider it done.'

She closed her eyes. 'Thank you.'

'But now you have to tell me something else that you want, because I *truly* feel as if I'm taking utter advantage of you.'

She glanced up to find him glaring at her. For some reason his outrage made her want to smile.

'What do I want?' she shrugged. 'I want to be out on the eastern boundary, helping with the weed eradication programme.'

Dylan stared at Mia and his heart thumped at the wistful expression that flitted across her face. He had a feeling that she didn't have a whole lot of fun in her life. Not if weed extermination topped the list of her wants.

If she agreed to his fake dating plan he resolved to make sure she had fun too. It would be the least he could do. There might be a lot of things he wasn't good at, but when it came to fun he was a grandmaster.

He rose. 'Okay, let's go and do that, then.'

'We?' She choked on her surprise.

He sat again, suddenly unsure. 'You'd prefer to go on your own?'

'Oh, it's not that. I… It's just…'

He could almost see the thoughts racing across her face. *It's hard work, dirty work, menial work.* 'You don't think I'm up to it, do you?'

'It's not that either—although it *is* hard work.' She leaned towards him, a frown in her eyes. 'Dylan, you run a world-class entertainment company. I'm quite sure you have better things to do with your time. I expect you're a very busy man.'

He shook his head. 'I'm on leave.' He'd taken it the moment Carla had announced her engagement. 'I have capable staff.'

And he couldn't think of anything he'd rather do at the moment than lighten Mia's load.

Inspiration hit him. 'Listen to this for a plan. If I become a volunteer here that might encourage Carla to become a volunteer too. If you get to work with her and build up a friendship then the fake dating stuff will be easier.'

Her frown cleared. 'There might even be no need for fake dating stuff.'

Maybe. Maybe not. He couldn't explain it, but the thought of fake dating Mia fired him to life in a way nothing else had in a long time. He'd relish the chance to find out what really make her tick.

'We need a cover story.' He rubbed his hands together. 'I can tell Carla that you piqued my interest—hence the reason I became a volunteer—and then we worked together, discovered we liked each other...and things have gone on from there.'

She screwed up her nose. 'I guess that *could* work...'

He grinned at her. 'Of course it'll work.'

She suddenly thrust out her jaw. 'I'm not going to spy on Carla for you.'

'I'm not asking you to. I'm asking you to become her friend.'

'If this works—if Carla decides she wants to be friends—then I mean to be a proper friend to her. And if that clashes with your agenda—'

He reached over and seized her hand, brought her wrist to his lips. Her eyes widened and her pulse jumped beneath his touch. A growing hunger roared through him. He wanted to put his tongue against that pulse point and kiss his way along her arm until he reached her mouth.

As if she'd read that thought in his face she reclaimed

her hand. He forced himself to focus on the conversation, rather than her intriguing scent.

'I'm asking nothing more than that you be Carla's friend.'

The way her gaze darted away betrayed her assumed composure. 'That's okay, then. As long as we're on the same page.'

'The same page' meant no fling, no relationship...no kissing. He had to keep things simple between them. There was too much at stake.

'Definitely on the same page,' he assured her.

Starting something with Mia was out of the question. She wouldn't last the distance any more than Caitlin had. His whole way of life was anathema to her.

A fist reached inside his gut and squeezed. Caitlin had left him at the absolute lowest point in his life. The devastation of losing his parents *and* her had... It had almost annihilated him. The shock of it still rebounded in his soul. The only thing that had kept him going was Carla, and the knowledge that she'd needed him. He'd found his feet. Eventually. He wasn't going to have them cut out from under him again by repeating the same mistakes.

He turned to find Mia halfway through a sentence.

'... I mean, we can give you overalls, but that's not going to really help, is it?'

She was worried he'd ruin his *clothes*? 'I have my workout gear in the car.'

She folded her arms. 'Along with a four-hundred-dollar pair of trainers, no doubt? I don't want to be held responsible for wrecking *those*.'

He had no idea how much his trainers had cost. But she was probably right. 'Couldn't you rustle me up a pair of boots?'

She gave a reluctant shrug. 'Maybe. Are you sure you want to do this?'

'Absolutely.'

'We'll need to register you as a volunteer. There'll be

forms to fill out and signatures required to ensure you're covered by the Plum Pines insurance.'

The more she tried to put him off, the more determined he became.

He rose with a decisive clap of his hands. 'Then let's get to it.'

She rose too, shaking her head. 'Don't say you weren't warned.

'What's going on here?' Gordon boomed, coming into the office just as Dylan emerged from the change room wearing the overalls and boots that Mia had found for him.

She sat nearby, already dressed for an afternoon of hard work.

She shot to her feet. 'Dylan—'

'Mr Fairweather,' Gordon corrected with a pointed glare.

'Dylan,' Dylan confirmed, deciding it would be just as satisfying to punch Gordon on the end of his bulbous nose as it would Thierry. He glanced at Mia and wondered when he'd become so bloodthirsty. 'I've decided to register as a volunteer.' He shoved his shoulders back. 'I want to see first-hand what my hundred-thousand-dollar donation will be subsidising.'

Gordon's jowls worked for a moment. 'It's very generous of you to give both your money *and* your time to Plum Pines…'

Behind Gordon's back, Mia gestured that they should leave. Dylan shrugged himself into full supercilious mode and deigned to nod in the other man's direction.

'Good afternoon, Gordon.'

'Good afternoon, Mr Fairweather.'

Dylan didn't invite Gordon to call him by his Christian name—just strode out through the door that Mia held open for him.

Behind him he heard Gordon mutter to the receptionist, 'Bloody trust fund babies,' before the door closed behind them.

Mia grinned as she strode along beside him. 'I think he likes you.'

He glanced at her grin and then threw his head back and roared.

'What on earth…?'

The moment Dylan rounded the side of their family home—affectionately dubbed 'The Palace'—Carla shot to her feet. Behind her a vista of blue sea and blue sky stretched to the horizon. It was a view he never tired of.

'Dylan, what on *earth* have you been doing? You're so… dirty! Filthy dirty. *Obscenely* dirty.'

He grinned. 'I signed up as a volunteer at Plum Pines. That was an inspired idea of yours, by the way. The place is amazing.'

She started to laugh, settling back into the plump cushions of the outdoor sofa. 'I have a feeling it's a certain Plum Pines employee rather than a newfound enthusiasm for conservation that has you *truly* inspired.'

He sobered. *What on earth…?* That was supposed to come as a surprise.

He managed a shrug. 'I like her.'

'I can tell.'

How could she tell?

She couldn't tell!

Romance had addled Carla's brain, that was all. She wanted everyone travelling on the same delirious cloud as she. It made her see romance where none existed. But he could work that to his advantage.

'I'm not sure she likes me.'

'And you think by becoming a volunteer it'll make her look upon you with a friendlier eye?'

'Along with my newfound enthusiasm for weed eradication.'

Carla laughed—a delightful sound that gladdened his heart. There'd been a time when he'd wondered if he'd ever hear her laugh again.

'She won't take any of your nonsense, you know.'

He eyed his sister carefully. 'Would it bug you if I asked her out?'

'Not at all.' She studied her fingernails. 'If you'll promise me one thing.'

'Name it.'

'That you won't judge Thierry too harshly based on today's events. He wasn't at his best. He's very different from us, Dylan, but I love him.' She turned a pleading gaze on him. 'Please?'

He bit back a sigh. 'Okay.'

'Thank you!'

He widened his stance. 'But I want to get to know him better before you two tie the knot.'

'That can be arranged.' Her smile widened. 'We can double date!'

Perfect.

'Perhaps,' he said, not wanting to appear too eager to share Mia with anyone else. 'Are you going to let him talk you out of volunteering?'

'Not a chance.' She laughed. 'I'm signing up first thing tomorrow.'

CHAPTER FIVE

MIA STARED INTO the mirror and rubbed a hand across her chest in an effort to soothe her racing heart.

You look fine.

Dylan had assured her that tonight's date—*fake*date— was casual, not dressy. They were meeting Carla and Thierry at some trendy burger joint for dinner and then going on to a movie.

She really needed to go shopping for some new clothes. She'd not bothered much with her appearance since getting out of jail. She'd avoided pretty things, bright colours, shunning anything that might draw attention.

She glanced back at the mirror. Her jeans and pale blue linen shirt were appropriately casual, if somewhat bland. The outfit wouldn't embarrass her. More to the point, it wouldn't embarrass Dylan. On impulse she threaded a pair of silver hoops through her ears.

For the last five days Dylan had spent every morning at Plum Pines, helping her dig out weeds. And for the entire time he'd remained unfailingly cheerful and good-natured. He'd never once made her feel as if he was counting down the hours until he'd met his side of the bargain.

He continued to flirt outrageously—not just with her but with all the other female volunteers too. It made her feel safe.

She shook her head at that thought. She had to remain vigilant, make sure she didn't become too comfortable around him.

She swung away from the mirror, tired of her reflection. The fact remained that she had limited wardrobe options and this was the best that she could muster. Brooding about it was pointless. Besides, she had more important things to worry about.

Like what on earth was she going to add to the conversation tonight?

She strode into her tiny living room and dropped to the sofa. She needed to come up with five topics of conversation. She glanced at the clock. *Fast!* Dylan would be here to collect her in fifteen minutes. She chewed on her bottom lip. No matter how much she might want to, she couldn't sit through dinner without saying anything. That wouldn't be keeping her end of the deal.

Dear God! What to talk about, though? *Think!*

A knock sounded on the door.

Her gaze flew to the clock. He was early. And she hadn't come up with even one topic of conversation!

Dylan hated to admit it, but he couldn't wait to catch a glimpse of Mia out of uniform. Not that he had anything against her uniform, but there was only so much khaki cotton twill a man could take.

In some deep hidden part of himself lurked a male fantasy he should no doubt be ashamed of, but... He'd love for Mia to answer the door in a short skirt and sky-high heels. *So predictable!* He had a feeling, though, that Mia probably didn't own either.

Still, he'd make do with jeans and a nice pair of ballet flats. That would be nice. Normal. And maybe away from work she'd start to relax some of that fierce guard of hers.

He knocked again and the door flew open. He smiled. *Bingo!* She wore jeans and ballet flats. With the added bonus of surprisingly jaunty earrings that drew attention to the dark glossiness of her hair. He'd not seen her with her hair down before. He had an insane urge to reach out and run his hand through it, to see if it were as soft and silky as it promised.

He curved his hand into a fist and kept it by his side. He'd meant to greet her with his typical over-the-top gallantry—kiss her hand, twirl her around and tell her she looked good enough to eat—except the expression in her eyes stopped him.

He made no move to open the screen door, just met her gaze through its mesh. 'What's wrong?'

Puffing out a sigh, she pushed the door open and gestured him in. 'You're early.'

'If you haven't finished getting ready I'm happy to wait. You look great, by the way.' He didn't want her thinking that he thought she didn't *look* ready. He didn't want her stressing about her appearance at all.

'No, I'm ready. I just… I don't do this, you know?'

'Date? Yes, so you said. It's not a date, Mia.'

Her living room was small. In fact the whole cottage was tiny. She'd told him earlier in the week that she rented one of the Plum Pines workers' cottages. There was a row of three of them on the south side of the reserve. From what he could tell, she ate, breathed and slept Plum Pines. He glanced around. Which seemed odd when she'd clearly taken few pains to make her cottage cosy and comfortable.

'Are you sure about this plan, Dylan?'

He turned back, frowning at her unease. 'What are you worried about?'

One slim shoulder lifted. 'That I'll embarrass you.' She gestured for him to take a seat on the sofa. She planted herself on a hard wooden chair at the little dining table pressed hard up against one wall.

She moistened her lips and he realised she wore a pale mocha-coloured lipstick. Desire arrowed straight to his groin. Gritting his teeth, he did his best to ignore it. For pity's sake, he'd warned himself off her—that should have been that!

He gritted his teeth harder. Apparently not. But, while he might find her attractive, he didn't have to act like a teenager. He needed to put her at her ease—not crank up the tension further.

'I can't imagine how you think you'll embarrass me.'

'I'm… I'm not much of a talker, but I know I need to keep up my share of the conversation tonight.'

His heart stilled before surging against the walls of his ribs.

She lifted her hands, only to let them drop back to her lap. 'I've been trying to come up with five fool-proof topics of conversation so that…' She shrugged again. 'So that I'm pulling my weight.'

In that moment he wanted nothing more than to tug her into his arms and hug her. He had a feeling that would be the last thing she'd want. He contented himself with leaning towards her instead. She wore a soft floral scent and he pulled it as far into his lungs as he could.

'I don't expect you to become a sudden chatterbox. It's not who you are. I don't want you to change. I like you just the way you are. So does Carla.'

Was she worried that the better they got to know her the less they'd like her? The thought disturbed him.

'It's just…you and Carla are so bubbly and fun. I should hate to put a dampener on that.'

She thought he was *fun*? A smile tugged through him. 'You mean Carla and I are noisy chatterboxes who dominate the conversation and won't let anyone else get a word in edgewise.'

Her eyes widened. 'I did *not* say that!'

He burst out laughing. After a moment she rolled her eyes, resting back in her seat.

'You must've worked out by now that Carla and I love an audience.'

She gave a non-committal, 'Hmm…'

'And you have to remember Thierry will be there, and no one could accuse call *him* of liveliness.'

'I'm not sure I want to be compared to Thierry.'

He tried a different tack. 'How did the school group go this afternoon?'

Her face lit up. 'They had a great time. It's so funny to watch them the first time they touch a snake or a lizard.'

He picked up the book sitting on her coffee table—a recent autobiography of a famous comedian. 'Good?'

'Yes, very. She's as funny on the page as she is on the television.'

He set the book back down. 'Did you hear about that prank the engineering students at the university pulled with the garden gnomes?'

She sent him an odd look. 'I saw the photos in the paper. It was rather cheeky…but funny.'

'What's a dish you've always meant to cook but never have?'

Her frown deepened. 'Um…veal scaloppini.'

'I couldn't help noticing that these cottages don't have any off-street parking.'

Her eyes narrowed. 'And…?'

'And I didn't see a car parked out the front, which leads me to conclude that you don't have a car.'

She folded her arms. 'That's correct.'

'Are you planning to get one?'

'Maybe.'

'When?'

Her forehead creased. 'What is this, Dylan? Twenty Questions?'

'There you go. There's your five topics of conversation, should you need them—a funny incident at work, a book recommendation, a local news story, does anyone have a recipe for veal scaloppini they'd recommend, and I'm thinking of getting a small to medium-sized hatchback—what should I get?'

She pushed her hair back behind her ears, all but glaring at him, before folding her arms again. 'How do you know I want a hatchback?'

'You're young and you don't have kids, which means you don't have to settle for a station wagon yet.'

She unfolded her arms, but then didn't seem to know what to do with them. She settled on clasping them in her lap. And then she smiled—*really* smiled—and it lit her up from the inside out. Her dark eyes danced and he felt a kick inside that should have felled him.

'Five topics of conversation—just like that.' She snapped her fingers. 'You managed it effortlessly. How can you make it so easy?'

'Probably the same way you can identify the difference between a bush orchid and a noxious weed.' He grinned, referencing an incident earlier in the week when he'd set about eradicating the wrong plant.

She continued to stare at him as if he were amazing, and he had the disconcerting feeling that he could bask in that admiration forever. He shrugged. 'Practice. In my line of work I have to talk to a lot of people. Though, if the truth be told, the sad fact is that I have a talent for frivolity and nonsense.'

'Good conversation is neither frivolous nor nonsensical.'

He waggled his eyebrows. 'It should be if you're doing it right.'

She didn't laugh. She met his gaze, her face sober. 'It's not nonsense to put someone at ease.'

His gut clenched up all over again. If he continued to put her at her ease would she eventually let him kiss her?

He stiffened. He and Mia were *not* going to kiss. They weren't going to do anything except find out if Thierry deserved Carla. Full stop.

This was nothing more than a case of opposites attracting. He and Mia were too different—too mismatched—to make things work in the long term. And he refused to do anything to hurt her in the short term. She'd been through enough.

By the end of dinner Dylan could cheerfully have strangled Thierry. The only contributions he'd made to the conversation had been negative, except when Carla had won a grudging concession that his gourmet burger was *'okay'*.

Mia, for all her worry, had been a delightful dinner companion. And nobody had needed to ask her if *her* burger was good. The expression on her face after she'd taken her first bite had made him grin.

Thierry had scowled.

From what Dylan could tell, scowling was Thierry's default setting.

When a lull had occurred in the conversation Mia had mentioned the book she was reading and asked if anyone else had read it.

Thierry had ignored the question.

Carla had invited Mia to join her book group.

Mia had kept her expression interested, but in her lap her fingernails had dug into her palms, creating half-moons in her flesh that he'd wanted to massage away.

She'd swallowed. 'Are you sure I'd be welcome?'

'All are welcome! We meet at the library on the first Wednesday of the month.'

'Well…thank you. It sounds like fun.' And she'd promised to read the following month's book.

Dylan had wanted to hug her. He hadn't known that asking her to befriend Carla, and the specific details involved, would be so difficult for her. The thing was, friendship didn't seem to be an issue at all. He sensed that both women genuinely liked each other. But going out and mixing with people was obviously a challenge for Mia.

He couldn't help thinking, though, that locking herself away and hiding from the world wasn't the right thing to do.

He'd taken his cue from her, however, and gone out of

his way to invite Thierry for a game of golf. Thierry had declined, saying he didn't play the game. Dylan had then tried inviting him out on his yacht, but Thierry had declined that too, saying he was too busy with work at the moment.

His heart had sunk when Carla had avoided his gaze. What on earth did she *see* in the man?

Now dinner was over, and they were finally seated in the cinema—Mia on one side of him and Carla and then Thierry on the other—Dylan let out a sigh of relief, no longer obligated to attempt small talk with his sister's fiancé.

It wasn't until the cinema darkened, though, that he suddenly remembered Mia's thin-lipped, pale-faced reaction to the nocturnal houses. *Damn it!* Did the cinema have the same effect?

He touched her arm and she started.

'Is being here uncomfortable for you? Is it like the nocturnal houses?' He kept his voice low so no one could overhear.

'No, it's fine. High ceiling…and it's cool. Those things make a difference.' Her eyes gleamed in the dim light. 'Actually, I'm really looking forward to the film.'

It made him wonder when had been the last time *he'd* relished an outing as simple as this one. Reaching over, he took her hand. When she stiffened, he leaned closer to whisper, 'It's just for show.'

It wasn't, though. He held her hand because he wanted to. He leaned in closer because he wanted to breathe in that subtle floral scent she wore.

When the movie started her hand finally relaxed in his as if she'd forgotten it was there. For the next ninety minutes Dylan experienced the romantic comedy tactilely—entirely through Mia's reactions. They weren't reactions visible in her face, but evident only via her hand in his—in the twitches, squeezes, sudden letting go, in her hand's tension and relief. He sat there spellbound as Mia worried for and cheered on the romantic leads. All of it rendered for him through her fingers.

What miracle allowed him to read the language of her hand so fluently? His heart surged against his ribs. He had to be careful not to let his fascination with this woman grow. *Very* careful. Nothing good could come of it.

When Dylan pulled up outside the front of Mia's cottage at the end of the evening she didn't invite him in.

She shook her head when he reached for his door handle. 'You don't need to walk me to my door.'

But what if he wanted to?

This isn't a real date.

He nodded. 'Right.'

She undid her seat belt. 'I just wanted to say…' She swung back, and even in the dark he could see the wariness in her eyes. 'I did have a nice time tonight, Dylan. Thank you.'

'I'm not after thanks. I want to apologise. For Thierry. Again.'

She shook her head. 'Not your place.'

He clocked the exact moment when she gave in to her curiosity.

'But why in particular this time?'

There'd been an excruciatingly awkward moment at dinner. Carla had asked Mia what the last film she'd been to see had been, and Mia had paled. Thierry had pounced with a narrow-eyed sneer.

'It might be more pertinent to ask, *When was the last time you went to the movies?*'

Dylan's gut had churned and an ugly heat had flushed through him.

Mia had answered with a quiet, 'It'll be over four years since I've been to see a movie.'

And the reason why—the fact she'd been in jail—had pulsed in all the spaces between them.

Dylan couldn't imagine Mia in prison—he couldn't make it make sense. But then he recalled her Spartan cottage and wondered if she'd actually left prison at all.

He rubbed a hand across his chest, trying to dislodge the hard ball that had settled there. 'Thierry went out of his way to make sure everyone remembered *why* you'd not been to see a film in so long.'

She glanced down at her hands. 'Dylan—'

'It wasn't only rude, it was unkind.' How could Carla marry someone like that?

Mia rubbed her hands down the front of her jeans. Finally she glanced at him. 'No matter how much you try to ignore it or justify it, the fact I've been in prison is not a small issue.'

He reached out to cup her face. 'Mia, you're more than your past. You're more than the mistakes that landed you in jail.'

Her bottom lip trembled. The pain that flashed through her eyes speared straight into his gut.

She reached up and with a squeeze removed his hand. 'It's kind of you to say that, but it's not what it feels like. It feels huge. It was a defining moment in my life. I completely understand why other people take issue with it.'

With that she slipped out of the car and strode up to her front door.

Dylan waited until she was safely ensconced inside and the veranda light was switched off with an unambiguous 'the night is over' conviction. With a sigh he didn't understand, he turned the car towards home.

Mia set her sandwich down and unclipped her ringing phone. 'Mia Maydew.'

'Mia, it's Dylan and I have brilliant news.'

The sound of his voice made her pulse gallop. She swallowed and did her best to sound cool and professional. 'Which is…?'

'I have an appointment with Felipe Fellini—the photographer Carla's been so hot for.'

That made her brows lift. She hadn't thought the guy did

weddings or celebrity functions any more. Still, the Fair-weathers had a lot of clout.

'She must be over the moon.'

'I haven't mentioned it to her yet. He's agreed to a meeting—nothing more. I don't want to get her hopes up until it's official.'

Dylan was certainly going above and beyond where Carla's wedding was concerned. Especially when he wasn't even convinced that it would go ahead.

Correction—he wasn't convinced that the groom was worthy of the bride. That was an entirely different matter.

'Mia, are you still there?"

'Yes. I… That's great news.' She tried to gush, but she wasn't much of a one for gushing. 'I'm very impressed.'

'Liar.' He laughed. 'You couldn't care less.'

'I want Carla's wedding to be perfect.' And she didn't care how surly, bad-tempered or humourless Thierry happened to be. With her whole heart she hoped he treated Carla with respect, that he made her happy…that he did indeed deserve her.

'That I *do* believe. The thing is, Felipe wants to meet at Plum Pines this afternoon—two o'clock, if possible. He's only in Newcastle for a couple of days, and his decision on whether or not to take the job apparently depends on the potential locations Plum Pines offers for wedding shots. He wants to start with the lily pond.'

In other words he wanted *her* to be available at two this afternoon to take Felipe around.

'That won't be a problem.'

She'd finished supervising the weed eradication programme last week. She was in the process of helping Veronica create an action plan for a particularly inaccessible area on the northern boundary. That, along with path maintenance, was what her week consisted of.

'Are you on your lunchbreak?'

She traced a finger along the wooden edge of the picnic table. 'I am.'

'Excellent! That means we can chat.'

She stared up into the eucalypt canopy above and shook her head. Dylan *always* wanted to chat. The sooner he got back to FWE and his usual work the better. He wasn't the kind of guy who liked sitting around and twiddling his thumbs, and she had a feeling Carla's wedding wouldn't have his full attention until he'd passed judgement on Thierry.

She suspected he rang her just to 'chat' in an effort to remove the sting of Thierry's incivility. Which was totally unnecessary. Only she didn't know how to say so without sounding ungracious.

'What are you having for lunch?'

She was having what she always had. 'A sandwich.'

'What's in it?'

She lifted the top slice of bread. 'Egg and lettuce. Why is this important?' Nevertheless, she found herself suppressing a smile.

'Are you having chocolate once you finish your *delicious* sandwich?'

She choked back a laugh. 'I refuse to have chocolate with *every* meal. I have a banana.'

'But you're missing a food group! You have carbohydrate, protein, a fruit and a vegetable, but no dairy. Chocolate is dairy. It makes for a rounded meal, Mia.'

She couldn't help but laugh. 'I'll see you at two, Dylan.'

She hung her phone back on her belt, a frown building through her. In the last fortnight Dylan had developed the habit of calling her a couple of times a week—always during her lunchbreak. Some days he didn't mention the wedding at all. She sometimes thought his sole reason for calling was simply to make her laugh. But why would he do that?

Was it really all for Carla's benefit?

Do you think he's doing it for your benefit? Do you really think he could be interested in you?

It was a ludicrous notion—utter wishful thinking. They'd set their ground rules. Dylan wasn't any more interested in a relationship than she was, and a fling was out of the question. But the wisdom of that reasoning didn't dissipate the heat building between them. It didn't quash the thrill that raced through her whenever she heard his voice. It didn't stop her from looking forward to seeing him this afternoon.

She bit into her sandwich. Since when had the prospect of a meeting become more attractive than tromping along solitary paths with loppers and a pair of secateurs?

She had to be careful around Dylan. *Very* careful. She couldn't go falling for his charm. Never again would she be a man's sap, his puppet. Not even one as alluring and attractive as Dylan. She'd sworn never to travel that particular path again.

Couldn't you just kiss him once anyway? Just to see?

The illicit thought came out of left field. She stiffened. No, she could not!

No *way* was she kissing Dylan. Any kissing was absolutely and utterly out of the question. That way led to the slippery slope of lost good intentions and foolish, deceitful dreams. She wasn't descending that slope again. She had no intention of falling into the pit that crouched at its bottom.

So...that's a no, then?

A definite no!

She wrapped up what was left of her sandwich and tossed it into a nearby bin. A glance at her watch told her she could manage an hour's worth of path maintenance before she had to get back to meet with Dylan and his photographer. Wrestling with overgrown native flora sounded exactly what she needed.

Neither the exercise nor Mia's resolution to resist Dylan's appeal stopped her every sense from firing to life the moment she clapped eyes on him that afternoon. It made her want to groan in despair.

No despair! She'd only need despair if she gave in to her attraction—if she handed her heart to him on a platter and became his willing slave. The attraction part of the equation was utterly normal. She'd defy *any* woman to look at Dylan and not appreciate him as the handsomest beast she'd ever laid eyes on.

Not that he *was* a beast. Not when he moved towards her, hand outstretched, a smile of delight on his face at seeing her. Then he was an utter sweetheart.

She couldn't stop herself from smiling back.

It's polite to smile.

Polite or not, she couldn't help it.

He kissed her cheek, his warm male scent raising gooseflesh on her arms.

'Mia…' He ushered her towards the other man. 'I'd like you to meet Felipe Fellini.'

She shook the photographer's hand. 'I've heard a lot about you, Mr Fellini.'

'Yes, yes, it is inevitable. Now *this*…' He gestured to encompass the lily pond and its surrounds. 'You must tell me that you have something better, something more original for me to work with than this.'

He strutted through the area in a coat embroidered with wild, colourful poppies, flinging his arms out in exaggerated disappointment while speaking in an affected American-Italian accent.

Mia stared at him, utterly flummoxed. Never, in all of her twenty-five years, had she ever come across someone like Felipe Fellini!

She moistened her lips. 'I…uh…you don't like it?'

'Ugh, darling! You *do*? I mean, *look* at it!' He pointed at the pond, the grass, a tree.

Behind Felipe's back, Dylan started to laugh silently. Mia had to choke back her answering mirth. 'I… I can't say as I've ever really thought about it.'

He swatted a hand in her direction. 'That's because you're

not an *artiste*. My sensitivities are honed to within an inch of their lives, darling.'

It should have been dismissive, but the words held a friendly edge and she suddenly realised he was having the time of his life.

She planted her hands on her hips. 'What's wrong with it?'

'It's a cliché. An utter cliché.'

'But isn't that what a wedding is all about?'

The question slipped out before she could censor it. She wished it back the moment both men spun to face her—Felipe with his hands up to cover his mouth as if utterly scandalised, Dylan contemplating her with those deep blue eyes, his delectable lips pursed.

'Dylan, *darling*, it appears I've met a creature I never thought existed—a truly unromantic woman.'

Dylan folded his arms, nudging the other man with his shoulder. 'I saw her first.'

Felipe spluttered with laughter. 'Darling, I'm not a ladies' man—but if I were…you'd be in trouble. I'd have her eating out of my hand in no time.'

Mia started to laugh. She couldn't help it. Felipe, it appeared, enjoyed flirting and games every bit as much as Dylan.

'Come along, you unromantic girl.' Felipe draped an arm across her shoulders with a smirk in Dylan's direction. 'Show me something worthy of my talents.'

Dylan fell in behind them with a good-natured grin. Mia led them to the utility she'd parked further down the track. One hundred and eighty hectares was a lot of ground to cover. They wouldn't manage it all on foot before dark.

Felipe discounted the first two spots Mia showed him—a forest glade of wattle, with low overhanging branches, and a pocket of rainforest complete with a tiny trickling stream.

'Clichéd?' she asked.

'Totally.'

'You don't know what you want, but you'll know it when you see it, right?'

Dylan's chuckle from the back seat filled the interior of the car, warming Mia's fingers and toes.

'I'll have none of your cheek, thank you, Dylan Fairweather. You, sir, are an uncultured and coarse Philistine.' He sniffed. 'I understand you have a *Gilmore* on your wall.'

For a moment Dylan's eyes met Mia's in the rear-vision mirror. 'You're welcome to come and admire it any time you like, Felipe.'

'*Pah!*'

At Mia's raised eyebrow, Dylan added, 'Jason Gilmore—like Felipe, here—is a world-class photographer.'

Felipe gave a disbelieving snort and Mia found herself grinning, Dylan and Felipe's high spirits momentarily rubbing off onto her.

'I've never heard of Jason Gilmore, but I've heard of Felipe. So I'm not sure this Mr Gilmore can be all that good. He certainly can't be in the same class as Felipe.'

Felipe reached out and clasped the hand she had on the steering wheel, pressing his other to his heart. '*I love* this girl.'

In the next instant he almost gave her a heart attack.

'Stop!' he screeched.

She slammed on the brakes, and even though they weren't going fast gravel still kicked up around them from the unsealed road. Before she could ask Felipe what was wrong, he was out of the car and moving with remarkable agility through the neighbouring strip of bush.

She glanced at Dylan in wordless enquiry.

He shook his head. 'I have no idea. But I suspect we should follow him.'

'This!' Felipe declared when they reached him.

Mia stared. 'It's a fallen tree.'

He seized her by the shoulders and propelled her to the tree, ordered her to straddle it. Next he forced Dylan to straddle it as well, facing her. Mia straightened and folded her arms, frowning at the photographer.

'Why do you frown at me?' He glared at Dylan. 'Why does she frown at me? Make her stop.'

'Uh… Mia…?'

'I can see that *you*—' she pointed a finger at Felipe '—will have no regard for Carla's dress.'

'*Pah!* This is art. If Carla wants art then she will need to make sacrifices. Now, do as I say and lean in towards each other.'

Whipping out his camera, he motioned with his hands for them to move closer together.

He heaved an exaggerated sigh. 'As if you're about to kiss. Mia, darling, I know you don't have a romantic bone in your delightful body, but you have a pulse, and you have to admit that your fellow model is very pretty. I need to capture the light and the landscape. Art is *work*.'

She glanced at Dylan to see if he'd taken Felipe's 'pretty' remark as a slight on his masculinity. She found him grinning.

He winked at her. 'You heard what the man said.' And then he puckered up in such an exaggerated way that any threat inherent in the situation was immediately removed. She puckered up too.

With the odd, 'Tsk!' as if in disapproval of their antics, Felipe set about taking photographs.

The flash made Mia wince.

'Headache?' Dylan asked.

'I just don't like having my photo taken.' The last time a flash had gone off in her face had been when she'd been led from the courthouse…in handcuffs. It wasn't a memory she relished.

As if he could sense her ambivalence, Dylan leapt to his feet.

'Darling!' Felipe spluttered. 'I—'

'You'll have to make do with just me as a model, Master Fellini. Run!' he muttered out of the corner of his mouth to Mia.

So she did. She shot to her feet and all but sprinted away, to stand behind and to one side of Felipe, in amongst the bracken fern.

She watched the two men's antics with growing enjoyment. Felipe barked out orders and Dylan promptly, if somewhat exaggeratedly, carried them out. He flirted with the camera without a scrap of self-consciousness. Felipe, in turn, flirted outrageously back.

Double entendres flew through the air until Mia found herself doubled up with laughter. It was just so much *fun* watching Dylan!

Without warning, Felipe turned and snapped a shot of her.

She blinked, sobering in an instant.

Dylan was immediately puffed up, all protective.

Felipe beamed as he stared down at his camera. 'Perfect!'

CHAPTER SIX

Mia swallowed. 'What do you mean, *perfect*?'

He gestured her over. 'Come and see.'

She didn't want to see. She wanted to run away to hack and slash hiking trails, to fill in potholes and be away from people with their unspoken questions and flashing cameras.

Dylan's not like that.

Dylan was the worst of the lot!

She forced reluctant feet over to where Felipe stood with his camera held out to her. Dylan moved across too, and she sensed the tension in his shoulders, in the set of his spine.

'You said you just wanted to test the light—to get a sense of scale and a feel for the locations, figure out how to make them work for you.'

'Darling, I'm an *artiste*. My mind, my eyes, my brain… they're always searching for the perfect shot.'

She went to take the camera from him, but he shook his head.

'Just look.'

She leaned in to look at the display on the screen. Her gut clenched up tight at what she saw.

Dylan leaned over her right shoulder. 'Holy cow…'

In the photograph, Mia stood knee-high in bracken fern, bent at the waist with her head thrown back, her mouth wide with laughter and her eyes crinkled and dancing. The entire picture rippled with laughter. She didn't know how Felipe had managed it, but when she stared at the photo she could feel delight wrap around her and lift her up.

He'd made her look beautiful.

She swallowed and straightened, bumping into Dylan. She moved away with a murmured apology.

'You see what I mean?' Felipe demanded. 'The picture is perfect.'

Her temples started to throb. 'It's a lie.'

'Art doesn't lie, darling.'

She was aware of how closely Dylan watched her, of how darkly his eyes throbbed as they moved between the image of her on the camera and the flesh and blood her. She found him just as disturbing as Felipe's photograph.

'Will you sign a release form, darling, allowing me to use that photograph in my next exhibition? This is *precisely* what I need.'

Her mouth dried. She had a plan. That plan was to remain in the background. *This* wasn't remaining in the background.

Her hands curled into fists. 'No.'

Felipe switched the cameral off with a sniff. 'That photograph could be the centrepiece of my next exhibition. And, darling, I don't actually *need* your permission. I was only being polite. This is a public place. As such, I'm free to take photographs of anything I please.'

Instinct told her that pleading with him would do no good. Her stomach started to churn.

'How much would a photograph like that sell for?'

She'd been aware of Dylan growing taller and sterner beside her. She glanced up and realised he'd transformed into full warrior mode. A pulse started up in her throat, and a vicarious thrill took hold of her veins even as she bit back a groan.

Felipe waved him away. 'It's impossible to put a price on a photograph like that. I have no intention of selling it.'

'Sell it to me *now*.'

Dylan named a sum that had her stomach lurching.

'No!' She swung round to him and shook her head. 'Don't even think about it. That's a ludicrous amount of money for a stupid photograph.'

He planted his hands on his hips. 'It's obvious you don't want it shown in a public exhibition. Let me buy it.'

She folded her arms to hide how much her hands shook. 'I don't want it hanging on your wall either.'

Why would he pay such a huge sum for a photograph of her anyway?

Because he cares?

She pushed that thought away. She didn't want him to care. She hadn't asked him to care!

As if he'd read that thought in her face, Dylan thrust out his jaw, his eyes glittering. 'Felipe, sell me the photo.'

She stabbed a finger at the photographer. 'You'll do nothing of the sort.'

Felipe turned to Dylan, hands raised. 'You heard what the lady said, darling.'

Dylan glowered—first at her and then at the photographer. 'Okay, let me make myself crystal-clear. If that photograph is ever displayed publicly I'll bring the biggest lawsuit you've ever seen crashing down on your head.'

Felipe merely smiled. 'The publicity will be delicious!'

Mia grabbed Dylan's arm and shook it, but her agitation barely seemed to register. It was as useless as rattling iron bars.

'You will do absolutely nothing of the sort!' she said.

His brows drew down low over his eyes, his entire mien darkening. 'Why not?'

'Because you don't own me. You don't get to make decisions for me.' She swung to Felipe. '*You* don't own me either. In a just world you wouldn't get to make such a decision either.'

Nobody said anything for a moment.

'Mia, darling…'

She didn't want to hear Felipe's excuses and justifications.

She turned towards the car. 'I thought art was supposed to make the world a better place, not a worse one. I think it's time we headed back.'

'Darling!'

She turned to find Felipe removing the memory card from the camera. He took her hand and closed her fingers over it. 'It's yours. I'm sorry.'

Relief almost made her stagger. 'Thank you,' she whispered, slipping it into her top pocket and fastening the button. She tried to lighten the mood. 'I expect for an *artiste* like yourself great photos are a dime a dozen.'

'No, darling, they're not,' he said, climbing into the car.

All the while she was aware of the brooding way Dylan watched her, of the stiff movements of his body, betraying...*anger*? It made her heart drum hard against her ribs.

'That photograph is truly unique, but I could not exhibit it without your blessing. I do not wish anyone to feel diminished by my art.'

She nodded. Felipe was a good man. So was Dylan. She was surrounded by people she didn't deserve.

'But if you should have a change of heart...ever change your mind...' He slipped a business card into her hand.

She nodded. 'You'll be the first to know.'

She didn't add that a change of heart was highly unlikely. She had a feeling he already knew that.

She glanced in the rear-vision mirror to find Dylan staring at her, his gaze dark and brooding. She had no idea what he was thinking or what he must think of *her*. Her pulse sped up again. Did he hate her after what she'd said?

She didn't want him to hate her.

She had a feeling, though, that it would be better for both of them if he did.

Dylan showed up at her cottage that night.

Without a word she ushered him in, wondering at her own lack of surprise at seeing him.

'I wanted to discuss what happened this afternoon,' he said without preamble.

'I don't see that there's much to discuss.' She turned towards the kitchen. 'Can I get you something to drink—tea or coffee? I have some light beer if you'd rather.'

'No, thank you.'

Good. They could keep this quick, then. She grabbed some water for herself and motioned him to the sofa, taking a seat at the table.

Dylan didn't sit. He stood in the middle of the room, arms folded, and glared at her.

She heaved a sigh. 'I'm sorry, Dylan, but I'm not a mind-reader. What exactly did you want to discuss?'

'I didn't appreciate your implication this afternoon that I was trying to own you. I simply felt responsible for putting you in a situation that had obviously made you uncomfortable. I set about fixing the situation. I don't see how that can be seen as trying to control you.'

She stared into her glass of water. 'I appreciate your intentions were good, but it doesn't change the fact that you didn't ask me my opinion first.'

'There wasn't time!' He flung an arm out. 'Where people like Felipe are concerned it's best to come at them hard and fast.'

'And what if I told you that your solutions were more horrifying to me than the initial problem?'

'Were they?'

'Yes.'

He widened his stance. 'Why?'

She stood then too, pressing her hands to her stomach. 'Ever since I got out of jail I've had one objective—to keep a low profile, to keep out of trouble. A lawsuit would create a hundred times more furore than an anonymous photograph in some exhibition.'

He straightened, his height almost intimidating. Not that

it frightened her. She sensed that frightening her was the last thing he wanted.

'Are you concerned that someone from your past will track you down?'

'No.' And she wasn't. That was all done with.

His hands went to his hips. 'Look, I understand your dismay at the thought of publicity, but what on earth was wrong with *me* buying the photograph?'

'I'm already beholden enough to you!'

'It's my money. I can do as I please with it.'

'Not on my watch, you can't. Not when you're spending that money solely for my benefit.'

He stared at her with unflinching eyes. 'You'd rather have let that picture go public then be beholden to me?'

She met his gaze. 'Yes.'

He wheeled away from her. When he swung back his eyes were blazing.

Before he could rail at her about ingratitude and stubbornness, she fired a question back at him. 'If Felipe had sold you that photograph, would you have given it to me?'

He stilled. His chin lowered several notches. 'I'd have promised to keep it safe.'

They both knew it wasn't the same thing. She could feel her lips twist. 'So, in the end, it was Felipe who did what I truly wanted after all.'

A tic started up in his jaw. 'This is the thanks I get for trying to help you?'

She refused to wither under his glare. 'You weren't trying to help me. What you're angry about is missing your chance to buy that picture.'

He moved in closer. 'And that scares the pants off of you, doesn't it?'

Bullseye.

She refused to let her fear show. 'I've told you where I stand on relationships and romance. I don't know how I can make it any plainer, but offering such a ludicrous sum for a photo of me leads me to suspect that you haven't heard me.'

'Some women would've found the gesture romantic.'

Exactly.

'Not me.'

He shoved his hands in his pockets and strode around the room. Mia did her absolute best not to notice the way the muscles of his shoulders rippled beneath the thin cotton of his business shirt, or how his powerful strides ate up the space in her tiny living room. He quivered like a big cat, agitated and undecided whether to pounce or not.

She knew exactly how to soothe him. If she went to him, put her arms around his neck and pressed her length against his, he'd gather her in his arms and they'd lose themselves to the pleasure they could bring each other.

The pulse at her throat pounded. She gripped her hands together. It wouldn't help. It might be possible to do 'uncomplicated' when it came to a fling, but refused to risk it.

If only that knowledge could cool the stampede of her blood!

He swung around. 'You might have your heart under lock and key, Mia, but you have no right to command mine.'

He wasn't promising her his heart. Heat gathered behind her eyes. He wasn't promising anything more than a quick roll in the hay, and they both knew it.

'You're forgetting the ground rules. We promised!'

'Just because I wanted that photo it doesn't mean I want *you.*'

But they both knew he desired her in the most primitive way a man could want a woman. And they both knew she desired him back. They were balancing too narrowly on a knife-edge here, and she couldn't let them fall.

She clamped her hands to her elbows. Wrapped up in his attraction for her were feelings of pity, a desire to make things better, and perhaps a little anger. It was an explosive combination in a man like Dylan—a nurturer with the heart of a warrior. He knew as well as she did that they could never fit into each other's lives. But hard experience had taught her that the heart didn't always choose what was good for it.

He leaned in so close his breath fanned her cheek. 'Did you destroy the photo?'

She wanted to say that she had.

No lying. No stealing.

She pulled in a ragged breath. 'No.'

'You *will* give it to me, you know.'

She shook her head. 'I have no need of your money.'

He ran the backs of his fingers down her cheek, making her shiver. 'I didn't say anything about buying it from you, Mia. I meant that eventually you'll give it to me as a gift.'

She wanted to tell him to go to hell, but his hand snaked behind her head and he pulled her mouth close to his own and the words dried in her throat.

Dear Lord, he was going to kiss her!

'The girl in that photograph is the woman you're meant to be. I know it and you know it.'

He was wrong! She didn't deserve to be that girl. She deserved nothing more than the chance to live her life in peace.

His breath fanned across her lips, addling her brain. She should step away, but she remained, quivering beneath his touch, hardly knowing what she wished for.

He pressed a kiss to the corner of her mouth. Her eyes fluttered closed as she turned towards him…

And then she found herself released.

'You want me as much as I want you.'

Her heart thudded in her ears. She had to reach out and steady herself against a chair.

'I don't know why the thought of being happy scares you.'

Disappointment and confusion battled with relief and her common sense, and it took a moment for his words to sink in. She pushed her shoulders back, but didn't lift her chin in challenge. She didn't want him to take chin-lifting as an invitation to kiss her.

'I am happy.'

Easing back from him, she seized her glass of water and took several steps away.

'Liar.'

He said the word softly, almost like a caress. He had a point. The thing was, she didn't need happiness. She just needed to stay on track.

She kept her back to him. 'I don't mean this to sound harsh, Dylan, but my happiness is not dependent on my sleeping with you.'

'I'm not talking about myself, here, Mia, or my ability to make you happy. I'm removing myself from the equation.'

'How convenient.'

'I think you're just as imprisoned now as you were when you were in jail.'

She spun around at that, water sloshing over the side of her glass. 'If you believe that, then it just goes to show how naïve you are.'

He blinked and then nodded. 'I'm sorry, I didn't mean that to sound glib.'

She didn't say anything. She just wanted him gone.

'Was it really so awful?'

She closed her eyes at the soft question. 'Yes.' She forced her eyes open again. 'I am *never* going back. And happiness is a small price to pay.'

His eyes throbbed at her words.

'I think it's time you left, Dylan.'

He stared at her for a long moment, but finally he nodded. 'Are you still okay for Saturday?'

For reasons known only to himself, Dylan had booked her and Carla in for a day of beauty treatments at a local spa. In the evening Mia, and presumably Thierry, were to dine with the Fairweathers at their coastal mansion.

Despite her curiosity about Dylan's home, she wasn't looking forward to either event. But she'd promised.

'Yes, of course.'

'Carla and I will collect you at ten.'

'I'll be ready.'

She'd need to go shopping before then. She had a feeling that she owned nothing appropriate for dinner at the Fairweather estate.

'You're very tense.'

Mia did her best to relax beneath the masseuse's hands, but found it almost impossible. She'd been poked and prodded, scrubbed and wrapped, and waxed and tweezed to within an inch of her life.

People did this for *fun*?

What she'd really like was to ask the masseuse to hand her a bathrobe, find her a cup of tea and leave her alone to soak up the glorious view on the other side of the picture window.

The spa was located on the sixth floor of an upmarket beachside hotel that boasted a sweeping view of Newcastle beach. It would be a relief and a joy to spend half an hour contemplating gold sands and blue seas.

'It's probably because of all the hard physical work she does,' Carla said from the massage table beside Mia's, her voice sounding like nothing more than a blissed-out sigh. 'Isn't this a gorgeous treat, Mia?'

'Gorgeous,' she murmured back. She might have made a no-lying promise, but in this instance the lie was lily-white. She had no intention of dampening Carla's enjoyment. That had been the one good thing about all this—spending time with Carla.

So Mia didn't ask for a bathrobe and a cup of tea. She gritted her teeth instead and endured a further forty minutes of kneading, pummelling and rubbing down.

'Change of plan,' Carla announced, waving her phone in the air as she and Mia moved towards Dylan in the hotel bar.

Mia swallowed and nodded in his direction, not able to meet his eye, glad to have Carla there as a buffer.

He turned on his bar stool. 'Change of plan?'

Mia glance up to find him staring straight at her. All she could do was shrug. She had no idea what Carla's change of plan entailed.

Meeting his gaze made her mouth go dry. Looking at him had the oddest effect on her. She should look away. If she could, perhaps she would. Instead, she gazed at him hungrily. He wore a pair of sand-coloured cargo shorts and... and a Hawaiian shirt that should have made him look silly, but didn't.

It made him look... She swallowed again. He looked like a Hollywood heartthrob, and as he raised the beer he nursed to his lips, a searing hunger burned a trail through her.

'Yes.' Carla finished texting before popping her phone into her handbag. 'Thierry's coming to collect me.'

He was? Carla was leaving her alone with Dylan?

Ooh...*horrible* plan!

'I've talked Mia into spending not just the evening with us, but the rest of the afternoon as well. So you'll need to take her home to collect her things. Thierry and I will meet you by the pool at four.'

With a perfumed air-kiss, Carla dashed out. Mia didn't know where to look. She glanced at her feet, at the window, at the bar.

'Would you like a drink?'

She glanced at his glass, still three-quarters full, and with a sigh slid onto the bar stool beside his. 'Do you think they'd make me a cup of tea?'

'I'm sure of it. English Breakfast, Earl Grey or Chamomile?'

'Earl Grey, please.'

He ordered the tea and without further ado asked, 'What's wrong?'

Straight to the heart of the matter. It shouldn't surprise her.

'Are you feeling awkward after the words we exchanged on Tuesday evening?'

She wished she could say no, but that lie *wouldn't* be lily-white.

'Aren't you?'

She doubted she'd ever have the power to hurt him, but she *had* disappointed him. She suspected women rarely turned Dylan down.

For heaven's sake, why would they? You must be crazy!

'Mia, you've every right to speak your mind. I might not like what you have to say, but there's no law that says you have to say things with the sole purpose of pleasing me. The only person you need to please is yourself.'

Did he mean that?

'I came on unnecessarily strong. I was upset…and I was prepared to throw our agreed ground rules out of the window.' He dragged a hand down his face. 'I'm sorry. You were right to hold firm.'

Her heart had no right to grow so heavy at his words.

'I know a relationship between us wouldn't work. And you've made it clear that a fling is out of the question.' He wrapped both hands around his beer. 'The thing is, I like you. It's as simple and as complicated as that.'

Her eyes burned.

'I'm sorry.' He grimaced. 'Can we be friends again?'

She managed a nod.

They were quiet while the barmen slid her tea in front of her. When she glanced back to him he sent her a half-grin. 'How did you enjoy the treatments?'

'Oh, I…' She hesitated too long. 'It was lovely.' She scrambled. 'Thank you.'

'You're lying!'

She debated with herself for a moment and then nodded. 'I hated it.'

His brows drew down low over his eyes, fire sparking in their depths. 'Was anybody rude or unpleasant…or worse?'

'No!' Before she could stop herself she reached out and touched his arm, wanting to dispel his dark suspicions. 'Everyone was attentive and professional. I couldn't fault anyone. It was me—not them. I just… I just don't like being touched by people I don't know.'

She closed her eyes and pulled in a breath. He must think her a freak.

When she opened them she found him staring down at her, his lips rueful. 'I'm sorry. It seems I'm constantly forcing you to do things you hate.'

She waved that away. 'It's not important. It's all in a good cause.'

'It does matter.'

'Let's talk about Carla and—'

'No.'

Mia blinked.

'Let me apologise. I'm sorry I took it for granted that you'd enjoy a spa day.'

'The majority of women would.'

'You're not the majority of women.'

That was true, but if she dwelled on that fact for too long she might throw up.

'Apology accepted.'

He sat back and she found she could breathe again. He had the oddest effect on her—she simultaneously wanted to push him away and pull him closer.

Maybe this time it wouldn't be like it was with Johnnie.

Maybe. Maybe not. But even if Dylan were willing she had no intention of finding out. She couldn't risk it.

She pushed those thoughts firmly out of her mind. 'Now, can we talk about Carla?'

He grinned. 'Absolutely.'

Despite her confusion she found herself smiling back. 'That was the one good thing about today. I enjoy spending time with her. She's good company.'

'Did she confide anything in you?'

Mia poured herself some tea and stared down into the dark liquid. 'She's totally in love with Thierry. Even if he *is* all your worst fears rolled into one, I can't see how you'll be able to stop this wedding.'

He dragged a hand down his face and her heart went out to him.

'But on the plus side...'

He glanced up, his eyes keen. 'Yes?'

How to put this delicately...? 'I've had some close experience with women who've been in emotionally and physically abusive relationships.'

His eyes went dark. 'How close?'

She knew what he wanted to know—if *she'd* ever been in an abusive relationship. She sidestepped the unspoken question. 'My father was abusive to my mother.'

'Physically?'

'Not quite.' Though that latent threat had hung over every fraught confrontation. 'But he was emotionally abusive until I don't think she had any sense of self left.'

'I'm sorry.'

'I'm not telling you this so you'll feel sorry for me. I'm telling you because I don't see any of the same signs in Carla that I saw in my mother. Carla is neither meek nor diffident. She's kind and easy-going, and I suspect she's peace-loving, but I wouldn't describe her as submissive or compliant. I don't think she's afraid of Thierry's displeasure.'

'Changes like the ones you describe in your mother—they don't happen overnight. They're the result of years of abuse.'

He had a point.

'There are men out there who prey on emotionally vulnerable women.'

He didn't need to tell *her* that. 'You think Carla is emotionally vulnerable because of what happened between her boyfriend and her best friend?'

He ran a finger through the condensation on his glass of beer. 'It's one of the reasons. She was only sixteen when our parents died. It was a very difficult time for her.'

'I expect it was a difficult time for you too. How old were *you*?'

'Twenty-one.'

Twenty-one and alone with a sixteen-year-old sister. Mia swallowed. 'It must've been devastating for you both. I'm sorry.'

He looked haggard for a moment. 'It was tough for a while.'

Understatement, much?

'And then there's the Fairweather name…'

She shook her head, not knowing what he meant.

'It's hard to know if the people we meet like us for ourselves or whether what they see is the money, the tradition, and the power behind the name.'

'But… That's awful!' To have to go through life like that… 'So that's why Carla didn't tell me who she really was when we first met.'

He nodded. 'I've not been sure of any woman since Caitlin.'

Her mouth went dry. 'The girl who broke your heart?'

'The very one.' He lifted his beer and drank deeply.

Leave it alone!

'You said she couldn't handle it when things got rough. Did she…?' She frowned. 'Did she dump you when you were in the middle of your grief for your parents?'

Pain briefly flashed in his eyes, and she went cold all over when he gave one curt nod.

She had to swallow before she could speak. 'I'm sorry.'

He sent her a self-deprecating half-smile that made her want to cry. 'I was head over heels for her. We'd been dating for two years. I had our lives all mapped out—finish uni, get married, see the world. I thought she was my rock. I wanted to be hers. I thought we were…not perfect—never that—but special.' He shrugged. 'I was a fool.'

The grief in his eyes caught at her. 'You were so young,

Dylan. You couldn't possibly have known she wouldn't last the distance. She probably didn't know either.'

He turned his head, his gaze sharpening. 'The thing is, I know you haven't the slightest interest in my money or my name. Funny, isn't it?'

'Hilarious.' She swallowed, understanding now, in a way she hadn't earlier, how serious he was about not pursuing a relationship. The realisation should have been comforting. 'But we both know we wouldn't fit.'

He stared into his glass. 'Building something worthwhile with someone is more than just being attracted to them.'

'Very true.' She wished her voice would emerge with more strength. 'You need to have shared values…to want the same things from life.'

That wasn't them.

He drained his beer. 'Luckily for us we have our ground rules to keep us on the straight and narrow.'

Her heart thudded hard. 'Amen.'

'Are you ready to go?'

She started to nod and then broke off to fiddle with the collar of her shirt. 'I have a problem.'

'Tell me,' he ordered. 'Fixing problems is my specialty.'

'Carla mentioned swimming and lounging by the pool. But the thing is… I don't have a swimsuit.'

He stared at her, and then he smiled—really smiled. 'That's a problem that's easily remedied.'

CHAPTER SEVEN

WHEN DYLAN PARKED the car at the shopping centre Mia removed her seat belt and turned fully to face him. 'We're not going to do the *Pretty Woman* thing in here, Dylan.'

He knew exactly what she meant and a secret fantasy—or not so secret, in this case—died a quick death.

He didn't argue with her. He'd already forced her into too many situations that she hadn't wanted this week.

He wanted to make her smile. Not frown.

He wanted to make her life a little bit easier. Not harder. And he had been making it harder. He couldn't deny that.

Then walk away now. Leave her be.

The look on her face when Felipe had snapped that photograph of her... It burned through his soul now. He'd wanted to make it up to her. He'd wanted to make things right. Nothing before had ever stung him the way her rejection of his aid had done.

She heaved out a sigh. 'Are we going to have to argue about this?'

He shook his head. 'Tell me exactly what you want to have happen in there.' He nodded towards the shops.

'I want to walk into a budget chain store, select a pair of board shorts and a swim-shirt, and pay for them with my own money. I then want to leave.'

Precise and exact.

'Can I make one small suggestion?'

She stared at him as if she didn't trust him and it occurred to him that he didn't blame her. His heavy-handed attempts to come to her defence last Tuesday hadn't been entirely unselfish. He'd wanted that photo.

He'd taken one look at it and he'd wanted it for himself. He couldn't even explain why!

It was pointless denying his attraction to her, but he had no intention of falling for Mia. It would be a replay of his relationship with Caitlin all over again, and he'd learned his lesson the first time around.

It was just... Mia had got under his skin. He hated the way Thierry treated her. He hated the way Gordon treated her. He chafed at how hard her life was—at the unfairness of it. He wanted her to feel free to laugh the way she had in Felipe's photograph.

It's not your job to make her laugh.

Maybe not, but what harm would it do?

He shook himself, realising the pause in their conversation was in danger of becoming too charged.

'It's just a small suggestion.'

She pursed her lips. He did his best not to focus on their lushness, or the need that surged into his blood, clenching hard and tight about his groin. If he stared at them too long she'd know exactly where his thoughts had strayed, and that would be a disaster. For whatever reason, she was determined to ignore the attraction between them. Today he didn't want to force her to face anything she didn't want to face or do anything she didn't want to do.

'Okay.' She hitched up her chin. 'What's this *small* suggestion?'

Her tone told him it had better be small. Or else. Her *'or else'* might be interesting, but he resisted the temptation. Today was about making things easier for her.

'I have it on pretty good authority that swim-shirts can chafe.'

She folded her arms, her lips twisting as if she thought he was spinning her a story.

'So you might want to buy a one-piece suit to wear underneath. And, while shirts are great for avoiding sunburn, they don't protect your face, arms and legs, so you might consider adding sunscreen to your shopping list too. And a hat.'

She smiled, and the noose that had started to tighten about his neck eased. 'I have sunscreen at home. I use it for work. But a new hat might be nice.'

He stared at that smile and then fumbled for the door handle. He needed to get out of the car now or he'd be in danger of kissing her.

'Let's go shopping.'

Mia looked cute in her board shorts and swim-shirt—a combination of blue and pink that set off the warmth of her skin and provided a perfect foil for the dark lustre of her hair. She'd look cute in the modest one-piece that he knew she wore beneath too, and while he'd be lying if he said he didn't care about seeing her in a bikini, a large part of him simply didn't care what she wore. That large part of him just wanted her to relax and be happy.

He glanced across. She reclined on a banana lounger, staring at her toes and smiling.

He moved to the lounger beside hers. 'What are you smiling at?'

Her cheeks went a delicious pink. 'Oh, I…'

He leaned closer, intrigued. ''Fess up.'

Her eyes danced. Not long ago they'd all enjoyed a rousing game of water volleyball in the pool, and it had improved everyone's mood—even Thierry's.

'This is going to sound utterly frivolous, but… I'm admiring my toes.'

He glanced at her toes and she wiggled them at him.

'I haven't had painted toenails since I was fifteen or sixteen…and the pedicurist has made them look so pretty.'

They were a shiny fairy-floss pink...and totally kissable.

'I think I'll sit here and admire them too. They're too cute for words.'

She laughed, and something inside him soared.

'I've had a really nice afternoon, Dylan. I just wanted to say thank you.'

'You're welcome. I'm hoping the fun continues well into the evening.'

She glanced across at Carla and Thierry, sitting at a table on the other side of the pool, a giant umbrella casting them in shade. 'Thierry seems a bit more relaxed today. Maybe pool volleyball is the secret to his soul.'

He found himself strangely reluctant to focus on the other couple's real or imagined issues at the moment. 'Would you like to see the Jason Gilmore?' At her frown he added, 'You remember. The photographer Felipe scoffed at?'

She hesitated, and then gestured out in front of her. 'Can it compete with this?'

He stared out at the view spread before them and then rested his hands back behind his head. 'Nothing can compete with this view.'

And it was all the better too for having Mia's toes in the foreground.

'You have a pool that looks like it belongs in a resort.'

The pool was long enough for laps, curving at one end to form a lagoon, with an island in the middle—a handy spot for resting drinks and nibbles. There was an infinity edge that had utterly bewitched Mia when she'd first seen it.

He nodded. The pool *was* amazing. 'But even better is the view beyond it.'

The Fairweather mansion sat on a headland, and the forest leading down the cliff obscured the beach below, but the Pacific Ocean was spread out before them in all its sapphire glory. Waves crashed against rocky outcrops and the spray lifted up into the air in a spectacular display of the ocean's power. It was elemental, primal and magnificent.

'We're incredibly lucky to live here.'

'You are,' she said, but her voice lacked any resentment. She glanced across at him. 'I suspect you work very hard for your luck.'

He gestured to the pool and the house. 'We inherited this from our parents.'

She gazed at him, her eyes moss-dark. 'And yet I bet you'd give it all up to spend just one more day with them.'

Her words hit him squarely in the secret, private part of himself that he let no one but Carla see. If only he could see his father again and ask his advice about how best to deal with his uncle. If only he could sit down with his mother and ask her how he could best support Carla. To have the chance to simply hug them one more time...share a meal with them...laugh with them. His chest burned with the ache of their absence.

'I'm sorry. I didn't mean to make you sad.'

He pushed himself out of his grief. 'Not sad.'

She shot him a tiny smile. 'You're a dreadful liar, Dylan.'

For some reason that made him laugh. 'I miss them. I don't know what else to say.'

'You don't have to say anything.'

With Mia he felt that might indeed be true.

'Is this photograph of yours in your bedroom?'

He stared at her, and a grin built through him. 'Did you think I was trying to whisk you away under false pretences?'

She pointed a finger at him, her lips twitching. 'I'm on to your tricks. You are *not* to be trusted.'

'Ah, but do you *want* me to be trustworthy?' He seized her finger and kissed it.

She sucked in a breath, her eyes widening, and it was all he could do not to lean across and kiss her for real.

If he kissed her now, she'd run.

And he was starting to realise that he'd do just about anything to make her stay. He had no idea what that meant.

'However, in this instance, madam, I'm being eminently trustworthy. The photo hangs in the formal lounge.'

She glanced at her toes, the view, and then at him. 'In that case I should like to see it.'

He rose, holding out his hand to her. She hesitated for a beat before putting her hand in his and letting him help her to her feet. He laced his fingers through hers, intent on holding on for as long as she'd let him.

'Why do you keep it in the formal lounge rather than the living area?'

'You'll understand when you see it.'

She left her hand in his and it felt like a victory.

The moment Mia clapped eyes on the photograph she understood why Dylan didn't keep it in the more informal living areas. Even distracted as she was by Dylan's touch, his fingers laced casually through hers as if he was used to holding hands with a woman, the power of the photograph beat at her.

In her entire life she'd only ever held hands with three men—her father, when she'd been very small, Johnnie, when she'd been very stupid, and now Dylan.

You're no longer either very young or very stupid.

She wasn't convinced about the latter.

She tugged her hand from his to take a step closer to the picture and he let her go—easily and smoothly.

'It's…awe-inspiring.'

She wasn't sure she'd be able to live with it every day. It was so powerful. She wasn't even sure where the power came from…

On the surface it seemed a simple landscape—a preternaturally still ocean with not a single wave ruffling its surface. In the foreground crouched a grassy headland, with every blade of grass as still as the water—unruffled by even the tiniest of breezes. But storm clouds hung low over the ocean, turning the water a menacing monochrome. Behind the photographer, though, the sun shone fierce, piercing the picture with a powerful light, making each blade of grass stand out in brilliant green relief. The contrast—so odd and so true—held her captive.

'What do you think?'

She had to swallow before she could speak. 'Your Mr Gilmore has caught that exact moment before a storm hits— before the wind rushes through and the clouds cover the sun. It's…it's the deep breath. It's like a duel between light and dark, good and evil.'

He moved to stand beside her. 'I feel that too.'

'And you know that in this instance the dark is going to win…'

'But?'

'But I can't help feeling it's not going to prevail—the dark is only temporary. Once the storm has worn itself out the sun will reign supreme again.'

They stood in silence and stared at it. Mia stiffened.

'It's about grief and hope,' she blurted out, unable to stop herself. 'It makes me feel sad and hopeful, and happy…and incredibly grateful, all at the same time.'

She turned to him and found all her emotions reflected in his face.

He nodded. 'I know.'

'It's the most amazing picture I've ever seen.'

'It's the second most amazing one *I've* seen.'

She'd started to turn towards the photo again, but at his words she turned back with a raised eyebrow. 'You've seen something to top this?'

'That photo Felipe took of you—it made me feel all of that and more.'

It was as if a hand reached out to squeeze her chest, making breathing all but impossible. 'Oh, I…'

She didn't know what to say, and the spell was broken when Carla burst into the room.

'Oh, Dylan!'

It seemed to her that he turned reluctantly. 'What's wrong?'

Carla wrung her hands, making odd noises in her throat, and Dylan's gaze sharpened.

Mia stepped forward to take her hand. 'What is it, Carla?'

Carla grasped her hand in a death grip. 'Oh, Mia, there aren't enough apologies in the world.' Turning to Dylan, she said, 'Uncle Andrew has just arrived.'

Her words seemed to age Dylan by ten years. It didn't take a rocket scientist to work out that there was no love lost between them and their uncle. He must be an utter ogre if his arrival could cause such an expression to darken Carla's eyes. As if…as if she might be *afraid* of the man.

Mia glanced at the photograph that dominated the wall and then pushed her shoulders back, aching to see Carla and Dylan smiling and laughing again.

'So…your uncle is a storm?'

Dylan's gaze speared hers. She sent him a small smile.

'I have a relative like that. I guess we'll just have to weather him.' She winked at Carla. 'Who knows? Maybe Thierry will charm him.'

Carla choked back a laugh.

Dylan glanced at the photo and something in his shoulders unhitched. He reached out and gave Mia a one-armed hug, pressing his lips to her hair. It was friendly and affectionate, not seductive, but it heated her blood all the same.

'Come on, then,' he said. 'Let's go and face the dragon.'

Over dinner Mia discovered that the elder Fairweather was everything she most feared—an intimidating authoritarian with views that were as narrow as they were strong. He was the kind of man who took his privilege for granted, but considered it his God-given duty to ensure that no one else in his family did.

Add to that the fact that Andrew Robert Fairweather was a Federal Court judge—he sent people to jail for a living—and Mia could feel her legs start to shake.

This was the person who'd replaced Carla and Dylan's

parents as role model and guardian? Her stomach rolled in a slow, sickening somersault. For all their trust fund money and fancy education, Mia didn't envy Dylan and Carla one jot. She found her heart going out to them in sympathy.

'It's past time I was introduced to this man you mean to marry, Carla. As you won't bring him to meet me, I've had to resort to descending on you unannounced.'

'You're welcome here any time, Uncle Andrew.' Dylan's smile didn't reach his eyes. 'Your room is always kept ready for you.'

'Humph!' He fixed his gaze on Mia. 'Who are *you*?' he barked.

Three years in prison had taught Mia to hide all visual evidence of fear. It had also taught her to fly beneath the radar. 'I'm Mia. Just a friend of Carla and Dylan's.'

He immediately passed over her to start grilling Thierry.

Thierry, it appeared, ticked every box on the elder Fairweather's list of what was desirable. As a self-made man in the world of finance, Thierry had power, position, and money of his own. They even knew some of the same people.

If Andrew Fairweather had expected Thierry to fawn he'd be sadly disappointed, but for the moment at least he didn't seem to hold that against the younger man.

Their exchange took the heat off the rest of them for a good fifteen minutes. Three sets of shoulders lowered a fraction. Dylan, Carla and Mia even dared to nibble at their thin slices of smoked salmon.

It wasn't until the entrée had been cleared away and a delicious risotto served that Fairweather Senior turned his attention back to his niece and nephew.

'Pray tell, Carla Ann, what are *you* doing with the education you've been so fortunate to have had? Frittering it away like your brother, no doubt?'

Carla glanced at Dylan. The older man had to be joking, right?

'Carla has no need to work for a living,' Thierry inserted

smoothly. 'She's in the fortunate position of being able to help others—a role she takes seriously and one I'm happy to support. Recently she's been busy working on charitable projects, including some important conservation work. I couldn't be more proud of her.'

Wow! Go, Thierry. Mia didn't blame Carla in the least for the look of unabashed adoration that she sent him.

Dylan glanced at Mia and raised an eyebrow. She could only shrug in answer.

'Well, what about *you*?'

His uncle fixed Dylan with a glare that made Mia quail internally. Silence stretched and she searched for something that would help ease the tension that had wrapped around the table.

She forced a forkful of food to her mouth and made an appreciative noise. 'This meal is really lovely. I'd... I'd like to become a better cook.'

Everyone stared at her. Her stomach curdled. She loathed being the centre of attention. She grasped the lifeline Dylan had given her on a previous occasion.

'I've always wanted to make veal scaloppini. I don't suppose anyone has a good recipe for that particular dish, do they?'

It was Thierry, of all people, who answered. 'I have a fool-proof recipe.'

Thierry *cooked*? She shook off her surprise. 'Would you be willing to share it?'

'Yes.'

Andrew Fairweather's face darkened. 'Dylan, I—'

'Maybe I could make it and you could all come to dinner at my place to try it?'

Carla finally got with the programme. 'What a lovely idea, Mia.'

From the corner of her eye Mia could see Mr Fairweather opening his mouth again, his hard gaze burning in Dylan's direction. She set her fork down.

'Maybe we should set a date?'

She couldn't seem to help herself, but she had a feeling she'd say anything to halt the malice she could see sitting on the end of the older man's tongue.

'What about Saturday two weeks from now?' Carla suggested.

'I'm free.' She had no social plans slotted into her calendar at all.

When she glanced at Dylan she found him smiling at her.

'Sounds great. If you're sure?'

Her stomach started to churn. She was very far from sure, but she couldn't back out now. 'If it's a disaster we'll just call out for pizza.'

She'd aimed for light, but even though both Dylan and Carla laughed it occurred to Mia then that nothing could lighten the mood around the table.

'Back to business!' Mr Fairweather boomed. 'Dylan, I want to know what you're working on at the moment.'

All her offer of dinner had done was delay the inevitable. His uncle fired question after question at Dylan—all of them designed to put him on the defensive, all of them designed to make him look small.

A frown built through her. But...*why*?

She glanced from Dylan to his uncle, trying to understand the animosity that crackled between them. Carla said nothing, just stared down at her plate of untouched food. Thierry met her gaze, but there was no help to be had there. His curled lip was directed at *her*, not at Fairweather Senior.

'You were given all of the tools to make something of yourself and you've wasted them,' Andrew Fairweather was saying.

No, he hadn't!

'I'm sorry I've disappointed you, sir.'

No! A hundred times no! Dylan shouldn't apologise to this man. In whose world could Dylan ever be construed as a failure? How could anyone conceivably interpret Dylan's achievements as worthless or lacking in value?

Would *no one* stick up for him?

Fairweather Senior slammed his knife and fork down. 'You could've done something *important*! Instead you've wasted the opportunities presented to you on trivial nonsense. You should be ashamed of yourself. You lack backbone and brains and you're—'

'You are *so* wrong!' Mia shot to her feet, quailing inside but unable to sit and listen to Dylan being run down like that any longer. 'What Dylan does is neither shallow nor trivial. He brings people's dreams to life. Don't you realise how important that is?'

'Important? He throws *parties* for a living. It's disgraceful!'

'You really mean to tell me you can't see the merit in what Dylan does?' Her daring and defiance made her stomach churn, but she couldn't stop herself. She turned to Dylan. 'How long have you had to put up with this?'

'Mia, I—'

She swung back to his uncle. 'Your nephew provides people with memories they can treasure for a lifetime. Dylan doesn't just "throw parties"—he doesn't just light sparklers and eat cake. He creates events that mark milestones in people's lives. He creates events that honour their accomplishments. He provides an opportunity for people to celebrate their achievements with their families, their friends and their peers. That's what life is about. It's not trivial or shallow. It's *important*!'

'*Duty* is what's important!'

Mia swallowed and reminded herself that she wasn't on trial here. Regardless of how much she displeased him, Fairweather Senior couldn't send her to jail simply for disagreeing with him.

'I agree that working hard and being a useful member of society is important—it's what we should all strive for.

And Dylan does both those things.' She lifted her hands sky-wards. 'Can't you *see* how hard he works? Can't you *see* how talented he is? He has a gift—he's a creator of dreams. And if you can't see the value in that then I pity you.'

She dropped her crisp linen napkin to the table. 'If you'll all excuse me for a moment…?'

She turned and walked out of the dining room. Every-thing started to shake—her hands, her knees…her breath. Letting herself out of a side door, she stumbled down a se-ries of steps and collapsed onto a low retaining wall that stood just beyond the light of the house. Dropping her head to her knees, she felt her shoulders shaking with the sobs she couldn't hold back.

'Shh…'

She found herself lifted and planted in Dylan's lap. His arms moved about her, holding her securely against him. His warm scent surrounded her.

'Why are you crying, Mia? You were magnificent.'

'I scared myself.' She hiccupped through her sobs. 'I… Men like your uncle scare me.'

'Men like that scare everyone. But at the moment I think he's more afraid of you.'

He said it to make her laugh, but she was still too shaken. She lifted her head and scrubbed her fists across her face. Dylan slapped her hands away and dried her face gently with the softest of cotton handkerchiefs.

'Look at me,' he urged gently.

'No.' She stared instead at her hands, but she couldn't prevent herself from leaning into him and taking comfort from his strength and his warmth.

'Why not?'

She pulled in a shaky breath. 'Because I know what I'll see in your face, Dylan, and I don't deserve it.'

'You don't think you deserve admiration and gratitude?'

'I don't.'

'Mia, you—'

'It was a man like your uncle who sentenced me to three years in jail. And he was right to do so. I'd broken the law. I'd taken money that didn't belong to me.'

She hadn't kept it, but that was neither here nor there.

'That's why my uncle scares you?'

She met his gaze then. 'I meant everything I said at the table. Every single word.'

His eyes throbbed into hers. 'I know.'

'But, Dylan, don't you see? All it would've taken was for Thierry to tell your uncle that I'm an ex-convict and that would've instantly negated everything I'd said.'

'Not in my eyes.'

No, not in Dylan's eyes. She reached up and touched his cheek. 'But it would in your uncle's…and most other people's too.'

He turned his head to press a kiss to her hand. She went to pull it away but he pressed his hand on top of it, trapping it between the heat of his hand and the warmth of his face.

'Does it matter what people like my uncle think?'

'Yes.'

'Why?'

'Because it means that whenever I stand up against some injustice, as soon as my background is known my protests have no effect, no impact. In fact it usually makes things worse—as if their association with me taints them. I might as well have kept my mouth shut.'

'You're wrong.'

The intensity of his gaze held her trapped. She couldn't look away.

'After you left just then, Carla announced to the table at large that she was proud of me. It's the very first time she's ever stood up to him.'

Her heart pounded against the walls of her chest. 'Have *you* ever stood up to him?'

'On Carla's account—but never my own.'

She couldn't stop herself from brushing his cheek with her thumb. It turned his eyes dark and slumberous.

Dangerous.

The word whispered through her, but she didn't move away. She liked being this close to Dylan.

'You shouldn't let him treat you the way he does.'

'I realised that tonight for the first time. I've made a lot of excuses for him over the years. He lost his brother, and he and my aunt provided a home for Carla when our parents died.' He shrugged. 'The family tradition of law and politics is important to him, but I had no intention of ever following that path. Letting him rant and rave at me seemed a small price to pay, but…'

'But?' she urged, wanting him to break free from all the belittling and bullying.

'But I hadn't realised until tonight how much I'd let his voice get inside my head. Somewhere over the years I'd unknowingly started to agree with him—started to define myself by his standards. But tonight you stood up and reminded me of why I do what I do. And I felt proud of it.'

She smiled. It came from way down deep inside her.

Dylan stared at her. His gaze lowered to her lips and the colour of his eyes darkened to a deep sapphire. A pulse started up in the centre of her.

'I want to kiss you, Mia.'

Her heart fluttered up into her throat. 'Oh, that would be a very, *very* bad idea.'

'Why?'

A part of her wished he'd just seize her lips with his and be done with talking.

Crazy thought!

'Because…' It was hard to talk with her heart hammering in her throat. 'Because I've made it clear where I stand in relation to romance and relationships.'

'And you think I want more?'

They'd set their ground rules, but…

'Do you?'

'Things change.' He spoke slowly, frowning.

His reply frightened her, and yet she didn't move away.

'I haven't changed.' She'd meant the declaration to sound defiant, but it came out whisper-soft and full of yearning. She couldn't drag her gaze from the firm promise of his lips.

'If you really don't want me to kiss you, I won't.' He trailed his fingers down her throat and along her collarbone. 'I meant to say earlier that I love your dress.'

The change of topic should have thrown her, but she grasped it like a lifeline. 'It's new. I bought it especially.' She hadn't been able to resist the raspberry-coloured linen dress once she'd tried it on.

'For tonight? For me?'

Her eyes met his.

No lying.

'Yes.'

His fingers continued to trail delicious paths of sensation across her skin. 'Are you sure your stance on romance hasn't changed?'

She couldn't look away. 'Positive.'

Liar.

'I still want to kiss you.'

She should move away, put an end to this insanity.

'And I think you want that too.'

Her heart beat so loud she thought he must hear it.

'Would you like me to kiss you, Mia?'

Her pulse thumped. 'I'll own to some curiosity,' she managed.

'Is that a yes?'

She met his gaze and nodded. 'Yes.'

CHAPTER EIGHT

MIA REALISED HER mistake the moment Dylan's mouth claimed hers.

She'd thought his first touch would be gentle, but it wasn't. It was sure and firm and a complete assault on her senses.

Dylan wanted to overwhelm her with sensation—perhaps in punishment for her 'my stance on romance hasn't changed' comment. He wanted to thank her for sticking up for him at the dinner table... And somehow both of those impulses cancelled out the underlying threat in the other and dragged Mia under as if she'd been picked up by a giant wave.

She wound her arms around his neck and held on, waiting for the crash to come as the wave barrelled her along... But it didn't slam her down as she'd feared. Dylan's arms cradled her, holding her safe, and in the end all Mia could do was sink into them.

He nibbled her bottom lip, coaxing her to open to him. And she did. She wanted to hesitate, to hold back, but she couldn't. His tongue laved her inner lips and something inside her unfurled. His tongue coaxed hers to dance and something inside her sparked to life, filling her veins with heat and her soul with joy.

Dylan deepened the kiss, kissing her so thoroughly and with such intensity that his name was wrenched from her throat.

He lifted his head for a moment, his eyes glittering, and she suddenly realised that the flirtatious charmer had been stripped away to reveal the warrior beneath. And every potent ruthless sinew of his being was focussed wholly on *her*.

It should have made her afraid.

But she wasn't afraid of him. All she had to do was tell him to stop. And she knew that he would.

One corner of his mouth lifted, as if he'd read that thought in her face. 'You think I'm going to give you a chance to *think*, Mia?'

Her heart thumped. 'Dylan, sex won't make a scrap of difference. I—'

The force of his kiss pushed her head back. One of his hands traced the length of her—slowly, lazily—and Mia couldn't help but kiss him back with just as much force, hunger ravaging her body.

She wanted this man.

If she couldn't have him she thought she might die.

And then his hand was beneath the skirt of her dress... and her hands were where they shouldn't be...

And somewhere nearby a door slammed.

Mia stiffened and pulled her hands to her lap. Dylan tugged her skirt down and put his arms around her, holding her close, just as Carla came around the side of the house.

She pulled up short when she saw them. 'I hope I'm not interrupting anything.'

Dylan laughed, the rumble vibrating through Mia's body in a delicious wave of sensation. 'Of course you're interrupting something.'

Carla waved that away. 'I wanted to let you know that Uncle Andrew has left. He's decided to stay at his club in town before heading back to Sydney tomorrow.'

Mia gripped her hands together. 'I'm sorry. I had no right to cause such a scene—'

'You were wonderful! I wish...' Carla hauled in a breath.

'I wish I'd had the gumption to say something like that to him years ago.'

'Carla,' Dylan began, 'you—'

'No.' She fixed him with a glare. 'You've always stuck up for me. I should've done the same for you.'

She turned to Mia. Mia tried to remove herself from Dylan's lap, but he held her there fast.

'The thing is,' Carla said, thankfully unaware of Mia's agitation, 'I've always been so terribly afraid of him. But tonight when you said you pitied him I realised you were right. And…' she shrugged '…now I find I'm not as afraid.'

Dylan frowned. Mia had to fight the urge to smooth his brow.

'I don't want you to be afraid of anyone,' he said.

Mia knew he meant Thierry.

Carla waved that away. 'I just wanted to make sure the two of you were okay. And to let you know the coast is clear.'

'We're fine.'

'And you, Mia?' Carla checked despite her brother's assurance.

'I'm fine too.'

'Carmen—' she was the Fairweathers' housekeeper '—is making ice cream sundaes.'

'We'll be along in five minutes.'

'Don't let him sweet-talk you into anything you're not ready for, Mia.'

'Cross my heart,' Mia promised, but that reminded her that Carla knew her brother's reputation. It reminded her that Dylan had a lot of experience with women while she had very little experience with men.'

Carla sent them a cheeky grin. 'But I *will* say the two of you do look cute together.'

Mia had to fight the urge to drop her face to her hands and weep. How could she have let things go this far?

Carla disappeared and Mia tried once again to rise from Dylan's lap, but his arms tightened about her.

'Do you really mean to ignore that kiss?'

His hand splayed against her hip, as if to urge her to feel what he was feeling.

'That kiss was amazing...intense.' His face darkened. 'It was a whole lot more than just a kiss and you know it.'

Her heart thumped. If she let them, his words could weave a spell about her. She couldn't let that happen.

'Yes,' she said. And then, so he knew what she was referring to, she added, 'Yes, I *do* mean to ignore that kiss.'

Her words made him flinch. Heat gathered behind her eyes and her throat started to ache.

'To punish yourself?' The question was scratched out of him—a raw rasp.

'No.' She refused to let the tears building behind her eyes to fall. 'To save myself.'

'I don't understand.'

The throb in his voice had her closing her eyes. 'And I hope to God you never do.'

This time when she tried to get up he let her.

Dylan watched Mia walk away and his heart pounded against the walls of his ribs. He wanted her with a savagery that frightened him.

He couldn't recall wanting Caitlin like this.

He couldn't recall wanting any woman with this kind of hunger!

He wanted to shred their ground rules to pieces—tear them up and burn them. He wanted Mia in his bed.

But do you want her in your heart?

The roaring inside him screeched to a halt. He swallowed. *No.*

But you're prepared to seduce her? To make things harder for her?

He shot to his feet. He wouldn't make them harder! He'd make sure she enjoyed every moment of their time together.

He'd make her laugh and he'd lavish her with gifts. He'd give her anything she wanted.

Except the quiet life she craves.

He whirled around, hands fisted. She was wrong about that. She should be living life to the full—not hiding herself in the shadows. She should be living her life like the woman in Felipe's photograph—full of joy and laughter. If only he could get her to see that.

If only…

He stilled. If he managed that, then maybe she'd rip up those ground rules herself and welcome some fun—some pleasure—into her life. It was worth a shot.

Thrusting out his jaw, he moved towards the house.

Mia sat at a picnic table, listlessly feeding a peacock what looked to be part of her usual lunchtime sandwich, and something in Dylan's chest tightened. It was four days since their kiss and she looked pale and tired. She looked the way he felt. It didn't give him the slightest sense of satisfaction or triumph.

He wanted her. His lips tightened. And she wanted him.

She had another think coming if she thought he'd give up. He wanted to know what she'd meant by saving herself, and he had every intention of finding out. Once he knew, he'd be able to develop a game plan for knocking down those walls of hers.

She half turned, as if she'd sensed his presence, dropping her sandwich when their gazes collided. The peacock immediately pounced on it.

Dylan forced his legs forward. 'It's just as well I brought these or you'd go hungry.' He dropped a couple of chocolate bars to the table before taking the seat opposite. 'How are you, Mia?'

'I'm okay.' She reached for one of the chocolate bars but didn't unwrap it, worry lurking in the depths of her eyes. 'How are *you*?'

He'd meant to tell her that he couldn't sleep at night for thinking of her. Instead he shot her a grin and winked. 'I'll be a whole lot better once I've eaten this.'

He seized the second chocolate bar and was rewarded when her shoulders unhitched a fraction.

'I'm glad you dropped by today,' she said.

He stared at her. For a moment he felt like punching the air. He didn't push her, though. He'd let her tell him why in her own time.

'Carla asked me to give you this.' He pulled a piece of paper from his pocket. 'It's Thierry's veal scaloppini recipe.'

'Why didn't she give it to me herself?'

He shrugged, hoping he hadn't given himself away. 'She said she was busy.' And he'd latched on to any excuse to see Mia. 'Maybe she thought I'd see you first.'

'Are you busy? There's something I'd like you to see.'

'I'm free as a bird.' Even if he hadn't been he'd have cancelled any appointment for her.

'Good. Come with me.'

She led him along a narrow track through dense native forest. Everything was hushed and serene. He marvelled anew that such a place existed in the middle of the city. Mia didn't talk and he was content to follow behind, admiring the dark lustre of her hair and the innate grace of her hips.

After ten minutes she slowed. Turning to him, she put a finger to her lips and then held down the branch of a Bottlebrush tree, gesturing for him to look.

He glanced at her, wondering what on earth she'd brought him here to see. He turned to survey the view and sucked in a breath. Moving closer, he held the branch for himself while Mia moved off to one side.

She'd brought him via a circuitous route to the far side of the lily pond. Just in front of him—no more than twenty yards away—stretched out on a picnic blanket, were Carla and Thierry. Carla's head was in Thierry's lap and he was idly combing his fingers through her hair. She laughed up at him at something he'd said.

Dylan's heart started to thump. He stared from his sister's face to her fiancé's face and back again. Eventually Mia's fingers wrapped about the top of his arm and she pulled him away. Pressing her finger to her lips again, she led him along a different path until they emerged into a rocky clearing. She sat on a boulder and stared at him with pursed lips.

He fell down onto a neighbouring rock, his mind racing. Finally he glanced across at her. 'I have *never* seen Carla that happy.'

She nodded, as if the sight of that much happiness had awed her.

'How did you know they were there?'

'I accidentally stumbled across them on Monday. I noticed Thierry's car in the car park a little while ago and figured they'd be there again today.'

'She's totally in love with him…and…and completely *happy*.'

'Did you notice the way he looked at her?'

He had. An ache stretched behind his eyes. 'He looked at her as if she were the most precious person on earth.' His shot to his feet and paced up and down for a bit before swinging back to Mia. 'A man who looks at a woman like that is never going to hurt her. He's going to do everything in his power to protect her, to cherish her…to make her happy.'

Mia nodded.

He started to pace again. Seeing Carla and Thierry together like that, so unguarded, it should put his mind at rest…

He collapsed back on his rock and Mia reached out to clasp his hand briefly. 'Dylan, you're not losing Carla. You're gaining a brother-in-law.'

'But he's such an unpleasant man!'

She sat back. 'I suspect the more you get to know him, the better you'll come to like him.'

Could she be right?

'I also think…'

He glanced up, suddenly on guard. There was something too tight in her voice, which was at odds with the casual way she ran her fingers along a tall spike of native grass.

'You also think…?' he prompted.

She rubbed her hand across her throat, not looking at him. 'I think our dating pretence is no longer necessary.'

She told you kissing her would be a bad idea.

He hadn't known it would have her bringing their relationship to such an abrupt halt!

There is no relationship.

But he wanted there to be. Not a relationship, *exactly*, but a relationship of sorts.

He was careful to keep his thoughts hidden. He didn't want to scare her off more than he already had—didn't want her retreating further. He hadn't got where he was today by revealing his hand too soon.

'You're probably right,' he said instead.

She seemed to tense up and then relax in equal measure. He ducked his head to hide his smile. Mia Maydew was one conflicted lady. If she'd just let him help solve that conflict…

'Please tell me you're not going to dump Carla as abruptly?'

Her head shot up. 'Of course I'm not going to dump Carla. Carla and I will be friends for as long as she wants us to be friends.' She folded her arms and glared at him. 'And, Dylan, I hate to point this out, but I'm not dumping *you* either. We were never going out to begin with. We were only pretending.'

'I wasn't pretending when I kissed you. And I don't care how good an actress you are, Mia, I don't think you were pretending either.'

She moistened her lips and swallowed. The pulse at the base of her throat fluttered like a caged thing. A ravaging hunger swept through him. If he kissed her now, here in this quiet, private place where they wouldn't be interrupted...

'Don't even think about it!'

Her eyes flashed fire. So much for not showing his hand. He stared at the ground and pulled in a breath, nodding. 'Sorry, I lost my head for a moment—let it drift to where it shouldn't have gone.'

He shoved his shoulders back and lifted his chin.

'Though if I'm ever fortunate enough to make love with you, Mia, it'll be in place where I'll have the opportunity to show you in every way I know how just how beautiful and desirable I find you. There'll be no rush. And your comfort will be paramount.'

Her eyes grew round.

He leaned in close. 'I've no inclination for a quick roll on spiky grass, where we'd be half eaten by ants and mosquitos or happened upon by unsuspecting hikers. When I make love to you, Mia, I mean for you to be fully focussed on me.'

She swallowed.

He brushed his lips across her ear. 'And when it happens I promise that you will be.'

She leapt away from him, glancing at her watch. 'My lunchbreak is almost up. I have to get back to work.'

He followed her to the main picnic area. It was awash with people enjoying the afternoon sun.

A question pressed against the back of his throat, but he held it in until they were fully surrounded by people. 'Will you give me one more fake date?'

Her hands went to her hips. 'Why?'

It would give him something to work towards. It would give him time to come up with a plan to overcome her objections to an affair.

'I want a chance to grill Thierry in a non-confrontational way, in a place that's not intimidating...and you *did* invite us all to dinner.'

Her shoulders suddenly sagged. 'I did, didn't I?'

She'd only done it to try and keep the peace, to try and head off his uncle's vitriol.

'You can cry off if you want. I can make your excuses easily enough. Nobody will mind.' He didn't want her looking so careworn—not on his account. 'Cooking for guests can be stressful if you haven't done it in a while.' He gave an exaggerated eye-roll. 'And I suspect I've stressed you out enough already.'

Her lips twitched. 'The cooking doesn't worry me. It's only for four—not fourteen.'

'What *does* worry you, then?'

She hesitated. 'My house.'

He couldn't gauge what she meant, but the way her hands twisted together caught at him. 'What's wrong with your house? I know it's small, but none of us are going to care about that.'

'It looks like a prison cell.'

He winced at her bluntness.

'It's bare and uninviting and…and I'm ashamed of it.'

'You've no reason to be ashamed of it. It's clean and functional. Neither Carla nor I care about things like that. And if Thierry does then he's an idiot.'

One slim shoulder lifted. 'I know it shouldn't matter. It's just… I have no talent for making things look nice.' She stared at a copse of trees. 'Maybe I could get a magazine or two, for tips on how to make it look a bit better.'

'I can help you with that.'

She raised an eyebrow, but he waved her scepticism away. 'You don't want a complete makeover. You just want it to look a little cheerier…a bit warmer, right?'

She nodded, but the wariness didn't leave her eyes.

'Look, I'm not an interior designer, but I've had to consult on set designs for concerts and themes for parties. Seriously, we could spruce up your little cottage with nothing more than a few accessories. I swear you'll be amazed at how easy it is.'

She didn't say anything.

'What's your budget?' he asked, so she'd know he wasn't offering to pay for anything, that he wasn't trying to bribe her.

She named a sum that, while small, would easily cover what she needed.

He rubbed his hands together. 'We can work with that.'

Her eyes narrowed. She folded her arms, her fingers drumming against her upper arms. 'What on earth do *you* know about budgets?'

It was a fair question. 'I had a crash course when I started up my company. And I'm given a budget from my clients for every event I take on. If I want to make money I have to stick to it.'

She glanced down at her hands. 'I'm sorry—that was ungracious. Of course you—'

'I'm a trust fund baby, Mia. If I chose I could live in the lap of luxury for the rest of my life without having to lift a finger. You're not the first person to question my credentials.'

She stared up at him, a frown in her eyes. 'You *haven't* chosen to live that way, though.'

He shrugged. 'I wanted something more. I wanted to create something of my own. Besides, the family tradition is not to sit idly back and rest on one's laurels. And as neither law nor politics interested me...'

'You decided to forge your own path?'

'And—as you so succinctly reminded me last Saturday night—I should be proud of that. And I am.'

She nodded.

'So, in return, will you let me help you decorate your cottage? We might not be dating for real, but there's no rule that says we can't be friends, is there?'

She chewed her lip.

Dylan's heart dipped. '*Is* there?'

'I...'

She moistened her lips and a sudden thirst welled inside him.

'I've largely kept to myself since…over the last eleven months.'

Would she *ever* confide the hows and the whys that had landed her in prison? He could search out police reports, court records—and he had no doubt that Thierry had done exactly that—but he didn't want to. He wanted Mia to tell him herself. It was obvious she regretted her crime. And she'd paid her debt to society. But her past still haunted her.

His heart surged against his ribs. 'Do you resent my and Carla's intrusion into your life?'

'No. I… I'd forgotten how nice it is to have friends.'

As those words sank in his mouth dried. 'I'm honoured to be your friend, Mia.' He swallowed. 'Carla would say the same if she were here. Neither of us take our friends for granted.'

'I know. It seems strange, when we're from such different backgrounds, that we can have so much in common.'

He rolled his shoulders in an effort to loosen the tension in them. 'Shall we go shopping, then? On Saturday? To spruce up your cottage?'

'I'm working till midday.'

'I'll call for you at one.'

'Um…'

She hesitated, and he knew it was a big step for her. 'Okay.'

He gave in to the temptation of kissing her cheek. 'I'll see you on Saturday.'

When he reached the end of the path he looked back to find her still watching him. He lifted his hand in farewell. With a visible start she waved back, before disappearing along a path between the office and a picnic table.

His hands clenched. Had anyone ever put her first? Fought for her? Put everything on the line for her?

He knew the answer in his bones—no, they hadn't.

Do you want to be the next person to let her down?

He *wasn't* going to let her down! He was going to show her how to live. When they parted company, she'd be glad they'd met. *That* was his objective.

Mia gazed around her tiny living room and could barely credit the difference a few knick-knacks made. She'd never had a chance to try her hand at decorating before. Her father had maintained a rigid view on what was and wasn't respectable—a line her mother had never crossed—and Mia hadn't even been allowed to put up posters in her room. She'd learned early on that it was easier to submit and keep the peace than to rebel.

When she'd met Johnnie his home had already been beautifully furnished. She'd been in awe of his taste. And in the two years between leaving home and moving in with Johnnie she'd lived such a hand-to-mouth existence there'd been no money left over for decorating the mean little rooms she'd rented.

And then there'd been prison. She'd learned to make do with as little as possible there. She'd left the place with the same attitude, but for the first time she questioned that wisdom. It was true that she didn't want to get too attached to material things—like Johnnie had. But it wasn't a crime to make her living space comfortable. It wasn't a crime to make it welcoming for visitors.

'Earth to Mia?'

She snapped back when a hand was waved in front of her face.

'You were miles away,' Dylan teased. He gestured to the room. 'Do you like it?'

'I love it.'

Shopping with Dylan today had been…*fun*. It had also been a revelation. She'd thought he'd walk through the shops and select the things she needed—like her father and Johnnie would have done. He hadn't, though. He'd asked her opinion every step of the way.

'I love the colour scheme you've chosen.' He planted his hands on his hips and glanced around. 'It makes everything so much lighter in here.'

'The colour scheme was a joint effort. I'd never have known where to start.'

He'd taken her shopping and asked her what colours she liked. She'd eventually settled on a china-blue and a sandy taupe. She now had scatter cushions and throw rugs in those colours on the couch, as well as a tablecloth on the table. New jars in a jaunty blue lined the kitchen counter, a vase and some knick-knacks sat on the mantel, and two beach prints in funky faded frames hung on the walls. A jute rug with a chocolate-coloured border rested beneath the coffee table and a welcome mat sat at the door.

Mia turned a full circle. 'It's made such a difference.' She clasped her hands beneath her chin and let out a long pent-up breath. A breath she felt she'd been holding ever since she'd proffered the dinner invitation. 'I no longer need to feel embarrassed.'

'A vase of fresh flowers here.' Dylan touched a spot on the kitchen counter. 'Maybe a plant on the coffee table or the hall table there, and the room will be perfect.'

Yellow-headed daisies in the kitchen and an African violet on the coffee table. 'I'll get them through the week.'

He grinned at her. 'Even better—it all came in under budget!'

His delight with himself made her laugh. She watched his face light up with pleasure as he studied the room he'd helped her to transform and her heart started to thud against her ribs.

Friends? She didn't believe in promises and words, but Dylan's actions today had spoken volumes. He'd given her his friendship willingly and generously. He'd treated her like a friend.

Now it was her turn.

CHAPTER NINE

'WITH US COMING in under-budget and all…' Mia's mouth started to dry. 'Well, I was thinking…how about I buy you dinner as a thank-you?'

Dylan swung to her, his eyes alert and watchful…hopeful.

'As a friend,' she added. She didn't want him getting the wrong impression.

'When?'

She strove for a shrug. 'This evening, if you're free.'

'I'm free.' He glanced down at himself. He wore a pair of cargo shorts and a button-down cotton shirt. So did she. 'Can we go somewhere casual?'

'Casual sounds good.' Casual sounded perfect!

'I know—gorgeous evening…end of summer and all that… There's this great pizza place down near the beach. It does takeaway.'

His face lit up and all she could do was stare. When—how?—had he learned to milk enjoyment from every moment?

'When was the last time you had pizza on the beach?'

'I… Never.'

'C'mon, then.' He took her hand and led her to the front door. 'That's an oversight that should be corrected immediately.'

* * *

'See? Didn't I tell you this was an inspired idea?' Dylan claimed a patch of pristine white sand and grinned at her.

Mia bit back a laugh and spread out a towel so he could place the pizza boxes onto it. 'I'll reserve judgement until I've tried the pizza.' She dropped two bottles of water to the towel too, and then turned to survey the view spread out in front of them.

They had another half an hour of light—possibly longer. The water reflected the last of the sun's brilliance in tones of pink, gold and mauve. Barely a breath of breeze ruffled her hair, and the only sounds were the whoosh of the waves rushing up onshore, the cries of the seagulls wheeling overhead and the laughter of a family group picnicking further along the sand. To her left, Newcastle's famous Nobby's Lighthouse sat atop the headland. Straight out in front of her was the Pacific Ocean.

So much space. So much room to breathe.

She pulled in a deep breath before turning to find Dylan watching her. With a self-conscious shrug she sat beside him. But not too close. She kept the pizza boxes between them. 'You couldn't have chosen a better spot. It's wonderful down here.'

'A perfect night for a picnic. Now, try a piece of this pizza."

She took a piece from the proffered box and bit into it. The flavours melted on her tongue and it was all she could do not to groan in appreciation. 'Good...' she murmured. 'Seriously good.'

They munched pizza in silence for a bit. The longer they sat there, the lighter Mia started to feel. Dylan reminded her of all the pleasures—big and small—that the world held. Even after almost eleven months she was still afraid of giving herself over to enjoyment.

'A penny for them.'

His voice broke into her thoughts.

'One moment you were enjoying all of this and the next moment you weren't.'

'Oh!' She swung to him. 'I'm having a lovely time. Truly.'

Her stomach clenched. She'd come here to tell him the truth.

So tell him the truth.

She finished off her piece of pizza and reached for a paper napkin. 'If you want to know the truth, I'm afraid of enjoying it too much.'

'Why?'

She couldn't look at him. 'In case I do something stupid and it's taken away from me again.'

He was silent for a couple of beats. 'You're talking about prison?'

She nodded.

'Is there any reason to believe you'll end up back there?'

Not if she remained vigilant.

'I find it hard to take my liberty for granted.' She grimaced. 'You don't understand how much you take it for granted until it's taken away. Prison is a punishment—it's supposed to be unpleasant. The thought of messing up and ending up back in there...' She shivered. 'So sometimes I find myself lost in a moment of enjoyment and then I remember jail and I wonder... I wonder how I could cope if I found myself back there again.'

He leaned towards her, drenching the air with a hint of smoky nutmeg. It mingled with the scents of ocean and pizza and she couldn't recall relishing anything more in her life. She wanted to close her eyes and memorise that scent, so she could pull it out and appreciate it whenever she needed to.

'Mia, you're a different person now. You won't make the same mistakes again.'

She wasn't convinced—especially on that last point. 'I think you need to know my story.'

'I'd like to know it very much.'

'It's sordid,' she warned.

She couldn't make this pretty for him, no matter how much she might want to. He just shrugged, his eyes not leaving her face. It made her mouth dry.

'Have you really not looked me up?' There'd be newspaper articles and court reports he could access.

'I wanted to hear the story from you—not from some so-called factual report that leaves out the truly relevant facts.'

She had a feeling that should have surprised her, but it didn't. She glanced down at her hands. 'I think I mentioned that my father was a...a difficult man.'

'Emotionally abusive to your mother?'

She nodded, fighting the weariness that wanted to claim her. 'When I was sixteen I finally stood up to him.'

'What happened?'

'He gave me a black eye and kicked me out.'

Dylan's hands fisted.

'I found temporary shelter in a homeless refuge and got work waitressing.'

'School?'

'I couldn't manage school *and* work.' She blew out a breath. 'That's something prison *did* give me—the opportunity to finish my high school education. It's my high school diploma that made me eligible for the traineeship at Plum Pines.'

'Right.'

She couldn't tell what he was thinking so she simply pushed on. 'When I was eighteen I met a man—Johnnie Peters. He was twenty-five and I thought him so worldly. I'd had a couple of boyfriends, you understand, but nothing serious.'

'Until Johnnie?'

'Until Johnnie...' She swallowed the lump that threatened her throat. It settled in her chest to ache with a dull throb. 'He swept me off my feet. I fell hopelessly in love with him.'

A muscle in Dylan's jaw worked. 'Would I be right in suspecting he didn't deserve you?'

She could feel her lips twist. It took all her strength to maintain eye contact with Dylan. 'The key word in my previous sentence was *hopelessly*.' She stared back out to sea. 'I had a lot of counselling when I was in jail. I understand now that there are men out there who target foolish, naïve girls. Which is exactly what I was.'

He reached out to squeeze her hand. 'You were young.'

She pulled her hand from his. 'When something looks too good to be true, it usually is. I knew that then, but I ignored it. He made me feel special, and I wanted to be special.' She gripped her hands together. 'He organised a new job for me—nine to five—where I was trained in office administration. It seemed like a step up. I was ridiculously grateful not to be on my feet all day, like I had been when waitressing.'

When she'd been in prison she'd longed for that waitressing job—aching legs and all. She should have been grateful for what she'd had. Content.

'He moved me into his lovely house and bought me beautiful clothes. He was a stockbroker, and I thought he could have his pick of women. I felt I was the luckiest girl alive.'

'He cut you off from your family and friends...controlled your finances?'

'My family had already cut me off, but...yes.' That was something she'd come to realise during sessions with her counsellor. 'Things seemed perfect for a couple of years. What I didn't realise was that he had a gambling problem.'

'What happened?' he prompted when she remained silent.

'He started asking me to deposit cheques into accounts that weren't in my name and then to withdraw the funds.'

'You gave all the money to him?'

'I gave him everything.' She'd been an idiot. 'Of course it was only a matter of time before I was traced on CCTV.'

'And Johnnie?'

'He was cleverer than I. He was never seen in the vicinity of any of the banks at the time, and he denied all knowledge.'

His mouth grew taut. 'The scumbag fed you to the wolves.'

She turned to him, the ache in her chest growing fierce. 'He was even smarter than that, Dylan. He convinced me to feed *myself* to the wolves. I told the police he was innocent.'

Anger flared in his eyes. 'How long did it take you to realise what he was?'

Her stomach churned. She'd told herself it would be better for Dylan to despise her than it would be for him to love her. A part of her died inside anyway.

'About four months into my sentence…when he hadn't been to see me…when he stopped answering my letters.'

'Then you turned him in to the authorities?'

She shook her head.

'You continued to let him walk all over you?'

She stiffened at the censure in his voice. 'Three things, Dylan. One—I had no proof. Especially not after the testimony I'd given in his favour. Any testimony to the contrary would've simply been written off as the ravings of a disaffected lover. Two—I needed to draw a line under that part of my life and move forward. And three—I deserved my punishment. Nothing was ever going to change that.'

'He *manipulated* you!'

'And I let him. I *knew* what I was doing was wrong. The first time I cashed a cheque he told me it was for his elderly aunt. The second time he said it was a favour for a work colleague. The third time he just asked me to do it for him, said that he was in trouble. I knew then that I was breaking the law, but I did it anyway. He never physically threatened me. I just did it.'

'But I bet the emotional threat of him breaking up with you hung over every request?'

It had. And she hadn't been able to face the thought of losing him. Talk about pathetic! 'I told you it was sordid.'

'Three years seems a long sentence for a first offender.'

She moistened her lips. 'I stole a *lot* of money.'

He stared out to sea and her heart burned at the conflict

reflected in his face. 'You made a bad choice and you've paid for it.' He turned, spearing her with his gaze. 'Would you make the same decision again, given what you know now?'

'Of course not. But we don't get the chance to live our lives over. We just have to find ways to live with our mistakes.'

'Shunning the simple pleasures in life won't help you do that.'

He had a point.

His brows drew down low over his eyes. 'Don't you worry about other young women he might have targeted?'

Her heart started to thump. Trust Dylan to worry about vulnerable women he didn't even know. She glanced down at her hands. 'Fourteen months into my sentence Johnnie attempted an armed hold-up on a security van. He wasn't successful. He was sentenced to fifteen years. I think the foolish young women of the world are safe from him for the moment.'

'Good.'

Neither one of them went back to eating pizza.

'Is that why you let men walk all over you?'

She stiffened. 'I don't let *you* walk all over me.'

His lips twisted, though his eyes remained hard. 'There's hope for me yet, then.'

'No, there's not! I—'

'You've let Gordon, Thierry and Felipe all treat you like you're worthless. Your father and Johnnie both treated you badly. Do you *really* hold yourself so cheaply?'

Her heart surged against her ribs. 'Neither my father nor Johnnie are in my life any more. Thierry doesn't matter to me one jot! Felipe *didn't* take advantage of me. And as for Gordon...'

Dylan folded his arms and raised his eyebrows.

'He has the power to fire me. Keeping my head beneath the parapet where he's concerned is the smartest course of action. It won't be forever.'

'There'll always be Gordons in your life in one form or another. Are you going to turn yourself into a doormat for all of them?'

'If I do it'll be none of your business!'

'Why tell me all of this, then?'

'Because if we're going to be *friends*—' she ground the word out '—eventually the press will find out who I am and my story will come out. And it wouldn't be fair to have the press spring something like that on you without preparing you first.'

He dragged a hand down his face.

'And...'

He stilled. 'And...?'

She didn't want to continue, but she had to. It was the reason she'd started this conversation. 'And I wanted you to understand why I have no intention of ever pursuing another romantic relationship.'

He stared at her, but she couldn't read the expression in his eyes.

'Because you were burned once?'

'Because I don't like who I am when I'm in love. I refuse to become that person again.'

He shot to his feet. 'Are you likening me to this Johnnie Peters?'

She shot to her feet too. 'Of course not!'

He stabbed a finger at her. 'That's *exactly* what you're doing. You're saying that if you let yourself be vulnerable to me, I'll take advantage of you.'

She could feel herself start to shake. 'This is about me, not you!'

'Garbage. I—'

He broke off when a bright flash momentarily blinded both of them. Mia realised two things then—night had fallen...and someone had just snapped their photo.

Without another word, Dylan charged off into the darkness.

Biting back a groan, Mia set off after him.

* * *

Dylan hurled himself at the shape that had emerged in the darkness, bringing the anonymous photographer down.

He tried to clamp down on the rage that had him wanting to tear things apart with his bare hands. He wanted to tear apart the men who'd let Mia down—her father, the despicable Johnnie Peters. He wanted to tear apart her mistaken view of herself as some kind of spineless push-over. He wanted to tear apart her view of *him*! Most of all he wanted to tear himself apart, and he didn't know why.

Don't tear the photographer apart. He's just doing his job.

'Fair go, Fairweather!'

Dylan pushed himself upright as Mia came running up. She shone the torch on her phone on the photographer, confirming Dylan's suspicions. A hard ball lodged in his belly.

'Percy Struthers. What the hell do you think you're doing, sneaking up on me again *now*?'

Percy had created a PR firestorm last year, when Dylan had been in charge of a Turkish sultan's sixtieth birthday celebrations. Percy had released a photo of Dylan and the Sultan's very beautiful youngest daughter, linking them romantically. It had been a lie, of course, but try telling *that* to an enraged Turkish sultan...

Percy Struthers was the grubbiest of the gutter press, and trouble with a capital T.

Mia had broken the law—she'd done wrong and she'd paid the price—but the world was full of immoral, unethical people who lied and cheated. Were *they* sent to jail? Hardly! Some of them were applauded and clapped on the back for it   like tabloid journalists and politicians.

'It's news whenever a new woman turns up in your life— you know that.'

'Give me the camera.'

With a sigh, Percy handed it over.

Dylan stood and indicated for Mia to shine her torch

on the camera. With a flick of his fingers he removed the memory stick.

Percy clambered to his feet, caught the camera when Dylan tossed it back to him. 'It won't stop the story, you know.'

'Without a photograph the story won't gain traction.'

They both knew that.

The photographer gave an ugly laugh. 'But one of us will eventually get a photo—you can't remain on your guard twenty-four-seven.'

Beside him, Mia stiffened. Dylan wanted to throw his head back and howl. This was her worst nightmare, and it was he who'd dragged her into it.

'I know who she is,' Percy continued. 'And I know what she's done.'

Her *absolute* worst nightmare.

'Aren't you afraid she's on the make? That you're simply her latest target?'

He felt rather than saw Mia flinch. A ball of fury lodged in his gut.

Don't rise to the bait. Don't give the pond scum anything. Don't feed the frenzy.

It hit him suddenly how much his name, his position, were black marks against him in Mia's book.

Percy gave another of those ugly laughs. 'An ex-con? *Really*, Dylan? What are you trying to prove? Or have you developed a taste for a bit of rough?'

Dylan reached out and took Mia's hand. 'I think we're done here.'

'Run along, darlin'.' The photographer smirked. 'We all know what you're after.'

And then he called her a name that no man should ever call a woman.

Dylan whirled around, his right hand fisted, and smashed him square on the nose. Blood burst from it as the man reeled backwards to sprawl on the ground. Pain shot up Dylan's arm.

Mia sucked in a breath, and even in the darkness he could see the way her eyes flashed.

Percy cursed. 'You'll pay for that, Fairweather.'

Mia tried to tug her hand from Dylan's but he refused to relinquish it. He towed her in the direction of the car instead. He had to get out of here before he did something truly despicable—like beat Percy Struthers to a pulp.

Mia sat in tight-lipped silence all the way home, only unfolding her arms to push herself out of the car once he'd pulled up at the front of her cottage. She slammed it with a force that made him wince.

He had to jog to catch up with her. She didn't hold the front door open for him, letting it fall behind her, meaning he had to catch it. But at least she hadn't slammed it in his face. He told himself that was something.

'You're...uh...cross with me?'

She turned on him, and her eyes flashed with so much anger the hair at her temples seemed to shake with it.

She seized his right hand and glanced down at it. 'Does it hurt?'

'Yes.'

'Good.'

She dropped it as if it burned her. Moving to the freezer, she took out a packet of frozen peas. Grabbing his hand, she slammed it on top of his grazed knuckles. It didn't really hurt any more, but he winced anyway, hoping it would give her more bloodthirsty impulses a measure of satisfaction. And he submitted when she pushed him towards one of her hard wooden chairs—not so hard now they sported pale blue chair pads.

She lifted his left hand and dropped it on top of the peas to hold them in place, then retreated to sit on the sofa and glower at him.

The silence started to saw on his nerves. 'You think I'm an idiot?'

'Totally.'

'He had no right to call you what he did.'

'You are *utterly* infuriating!' Her hands balled into fists. 'What he called me was despicable, but the best thing you could've done was walk away without giving him the satisfaction of reacting.' She shot to her feet and started to pace. 'Oh, but, *no*—you couldn't manage that, could you? No! Your honour demanded reparation for the lady—regardless of how much more difficult you'd be making it for said lady!'

He shifted on the chair. 'I…uh…'

'The story will break in the tabloids, the ugliest accusations will be made, and I'll be hounded by reporters and photographers at work. *Hell!*' She flung her arms out. 'Just wait until Gordon catches wind of this. I'll be out on my ear.' She swung to him, thumping a hand to her chest. 'I *need* to finish this traineeship. I need a decent qualification so I can get a job.'

'I've already told you—come and work for me.'

'I don't *want* to work for you!'

Her rejection stung. He shot to his feet then too. 'That's right—you'd rather bury yourself in some godforsaken place where you can sentence yourself to a life of solitary confinement.'

'That's *my* decision to make.'

He wanted to hurl the peas across the room. Except he didn't want to ruin the pretty new furnishings. He had to settle for dropping them in the sink instead.

He moved back into the middle of the room. 'I have no intention of making light of your experiences with the criminal justice system, but you're letting one experience colour your entire life.' That hard lump of anger in his chest rose up into his throat. 'And I am *not* Johnnie Peters.'

Her entire frame shook. 'I told you—this is about *me*. Not you.' She didn't yell, but her words speared through him as if they'd come at him at great volume. 'You *punched* a man tonight, Dylan. That photographer can have you charged with assault. He'd be within his rights.'

It was true. It had been foolish to react. He couldn't find it in himself to regret it, though.

'And you made *me* an eye witness to the event.'

He swung back to meet her gaze. What he saw there made his heart burn.

'If I were in love with you, and you asked me to lie to the police about what had happened tonight...'

She didn't finish the sentence, but her pallor made his stomach churn.

'You're afraid you'd perjure yourself for me?'

'If I fell in love with you, Dylan, I'm afraid I'd risk everything again.'

He reached out to curl his fingers around her shoulders. 'I would *never* ask that of you.'

She moved away until his hands dropped back to his sides. 'The best way for me to avoid that kind of temptation is to avoid romantic attachments altogether. All I want is a quiet life. It doesn't seem too much to ask. It doesn't seem like such a big sacrifice to make.'

Ice sped through his veins. 'You're mistaken if you think living a half-life isn't a sacrifice. It'll keep you out of jail, it'll keep you out of trouble, but there are worse things than jail.'

She blinked, as if that wasn't a thought that had ever occurred to her.

'Living a life without love is one of them. And here's another thing for you to think about. If I fell in love with *you*—' he pointed a finger at her '—who's to say you wouldn't have the same power over me that Johnnie had over you? Who's to say you wouldn't force me to turn my back on my principles?'

The words spilled from him with an uncanny truth that left him reeling.

Her mouth dropped open.

He forged on, not understanding what was happening to him. 'Do you think I'd lie, steal or perjure myself for you?'

Her hands twisted together. 'You might lie for me…if it wasn't a big lie.'

He widened his stance. 'But the rest?'

She bit her lip and finally shook her head. 'No.'

'What makes you think *you* would, then?'

'My past tells me I'm weak.'

'Do you really think three years in prison—with all the education and counselling you received—hasn't made you stronger?'

She still labelled herself as weak-willed and easy to manipulate. He understood her fear of prison, and her determination never to find herself back behind bars, but she was wrong. She might let people like Gordon push her around, but she was as strong as one of the Plum Pines the reserve was named after.

Behind the dark moss of her eyes he could see her mind racing. He mightn't have convinced her. *Yet.* But he'd given her something to think about.

He snaked his hand behind her head and drew her face close to his.

'What are you doing?' she squeaked.

'I'm giving you something else to think about. Do you *really* want to live without this, Mia?'

He wanted to slam his lips to hers and kiss her with all the pent-up frustration tearing at his soul. He didn't. She'd tensed, ready to resist such an assault. And he didn't want to hurt her. If she'd let him he'd do everything he could to make her happy.

He touched his lips to hers gently, slowly exploring the lush lines of her mouth—savouring her. He poured all of himself into the kiss, wanting to give her as much pleasure as he could.

With a shiver and a sigh she sank against him, her hands fisting in his shirt. At his gentle demand she opened up to him and he felt as if he was home. Murmuring her name, he moved to gather her close—only to find a hand planted on his chest, pushing him away.

'Stop.'

He released her immediately.

Her chest rose and fell as if she'd been running. 'You shouldn't be kissing me.'

He couldn't think of anything he'd rather do.

'What you should be doing is readying yourself for the PR disaster that's about to hit.'

He remained silent until she lifted her gaze to his. 'I promise you won't lose your job.'

She snorted her disbelief. 'Will you please warn Carla too? I think it'd be a good idea if you told her all that I told you tonight.'

'You want Carla to know?'

'It seems only fair.'

'No.' He refused to be a party to her shutting herself off from people. 'If you're truly her friend, Mia, then *you* tell her.'

With that, he spun on his heel and left.

Dylan stumbled down Mia's front steps, feeling as if he'd descended a drop of a thousand feet. He put out a hand to steady himself, but there was nothing to grab on to. He stood there swaying, praying he'd find his balance soon.

What had just happened?

Idiot!

The word screamed over and over in his mind, but he didn't know why.

What was so idiotic about anything he'd done tonight? Mia might think him an idiot for punching Percy Struthers, but the man had deserved it. Given the chance, he'd do it again! And he wasn't an idiot for refusing to be labelled as another Johnnie Peters either.

Pain shot into his jaw from clenching his teeth too hard. He was *nothing* like Johnnie Peters!

He lurched over to his car and flung the door open, but he didn't get in.

He wasn't an idiot for fighting against Mia's mistaken view of herself. She wasn't weak! She was one of the strongest women he knew.

Stronger than Caitlin.

He froze. Where had *that* come from?

But… Mia *was* stronger than Caitlin.

His mouth dried, and his heart was pounding so hard it sent nausea swirling through him. Mia was *exactly* the kind of woman who'd go the distance with a man—who'd take the good times with the bad, who'd weather the storms. Mia wouldn't turn tail and run at the first sign of trouble. If things got tough she'd dig her heels in and wait it out.

Idiot!

It finally hit him why that word kept going round and round in his mind. He collapsed on to the car seat. He'd been telling himself all this time that what he wanted with Mia was an affair, but that was a lie.

He wanted it all. *He loved her.* He wanted a chance to build a life with her.

His vision darkened. He raked his hands through his hair. All this time he'd thought he'd been keeping his heart safe… and yet the whole time he'd been falling in love with her.

His hands clenched about the steering wheel. He would *not* give up! Mia had told his uncle that he, Dylan, made dreams come true. Was there the slightest chance on earth that he could make *her* dreams come true?

If he wanted to win her heart he had to find out.

CHAPTER TEN

THE STORY DIDN'T break on Monday or Tuesday. It didn't break on Wednesday or Thursday either. There wasn't a single item in the newspapers about Dylan, let alone any shady ex-convict women he might be dating.

Not that they *were* dating.

Even if he'd made it clear that he'd like to be.

Mia's wilful heart leapt at the thought, avoiding all her attempts to squash its exuberance.

She'd finally gathered up the courage to ring Carla on Tuesday night. Carla had claimed she didn't care about Mia's history—that she only cared about the kind of person Mia was now. Mia had even believed her.

She hadn't seen Dylan all week. He hadn't dropped by Plum Pines during her lunchbreak. He hadn't rung her for no reason at all other than to talk nonsense until she started to laugh in spite of herself. He hadn't even rung to talk about the wedding.

Despite her best intentions, she missed him.

She didn't just miss him—she *ached* for him.

On Friday morning, when it was barely light, she rushed the one and a half kilometres to the nearest newsagent's to buy a newspaper. Again, nothing.

Saturday dawned—the day of her dinner party—and still no scandal broke. She could hardly imagine what strings

Dylan had pulled to hush up the story. Could she start to breathe more easily?

It didn't make the memory of their encounter with the photographer fade, though. She physically flinched whenever she recalled the moment Dylan had punched the other man. Was he *crazy*? He could have been hauled off in a paddy wagon and thrown in a cell overnight! All because someone had called her a bad name.

Couldn't he see that for the rest of her life there'd be people who'd be happy to call her bad names? What would he do—punch them *all* on the nose?

Dylan deserved better than that.

So do you.

The thought whispered through her and she had to sink down into the nearest chair. Her heart thumped, the pulse in her throat pounded and her temples throbbed.

There are worse things than prison.

Dylan was right.

Shame, sharp and hot, engulfed her. She'd stolen money from people—people who hadn't deserved it. Knowing she was capable of that—living with that knowledge—was the worst thing of all. She'd willingly spend another three years in prison if it would rid her of the taint. But it wouldn't. Nothing would. Saying sorry to the people she'd hurt, doing her jail time, being a model prisoner, having the counselling— none of that had helped.

The only way she could ensure she never did something like that again was to stay away from people as much as she could.

Heat burned the backs of her eyes. She pressed a fist to her mouth. She wanted to believe Dylan—believe that she'd changed, become stronger, that no one could manipulate her now. His face rose up in her mind…a beautiful dream she'd kept telling herself was out of reach. Her every atom yearned towards him.

With a half-sob, she closed her eyes. She couldn't reach for that dream until she was certain she'd changed.

But how could she ever be certain of that?

Mia glanced at the plate of nibbles she'd set on the coffee table—some nice cheese and fancy crackers, along with some fat feta-stuffed olives. Should she add some grapes to the platter?

She clasped and unclasped her hands. She wasn't serving an entrée—just a main and a dessert…and these pre-dinner nibbles.

She peered into the refrigerator to check on the individual crème-brûlées she'd prepared earlier. What if they'd spoiled?

They hadn't.

She glanced at the wine. What if she'd chosen the wrong sort? She knew nothing about wine. The man at the liquor store had been helpful, but still…

What if nobody wanted wine? What if they wanted something she didn't have? She'd stocked up on mineral water and cola. She'd filled umpteen ice cube trays, so there'd be plenty of ice, but… She hadn't thought to buy port. What if someone wanted an after-dinner port? Or sherry!

She twisted her hands together. What if she ruined the veal scaloppini?

We'll call out for pizza.

What if she spilled a whole bottle of wine?

We'll mop it up.

What if—?

Relax.

The voice in her head sounded suspiciously like Dylan's. Funnily enough, it *did* help calm her panic.

It's just a dinner for friends. Nothing to get het up about.

A knock sounded at the front door and her heart immediately leapt into her throat.

They were twenty minutes early!

Does it matter?

Yes. No. She didn't know.

She wiped her palms down her pretty pink summer dress—another extravagant spur-of-the-moment purchase. She'd been making a few of those since she'd met Dylan—not that she could find it in herself to regret them.

Pulling in a breath, she went to answer it. Dylan stared at her from behind the screen. He held a bottle of wine and a bunch of flowers, but she barely noticed them against the intensity of his burning blue eyes.

Swallowing, she unlatched the screen and pushed it open. 'Come in.'

He kissed her cheek—all formality—and handed her the wine and flowers. 'Gifts for the hostess.'

She swallowed again, her senses drenched with the nutmeg scent of him. 'Thank you.'

While he might be physically close, his reserve made him seem a million miles away. Her fingers tightened around the stems of the flowers. She had no idea how to breach that distance. She wasn't even sure she should attempt it.

'I didn't know if you'd come.' She moved behind the kitchen counter to find a vase for the flowers—yellow-headed daisies.

'I'd have let you know if I couldn't make it.'

Of course he would. He had impeccable manners.

She glanced up to find him scrutinising her living room, a frown—small but unmistakable—settling over his features.

She set the vase of flowers on the kitchen bench and walked across. 'What's wrong?' Maybe he hated cheese and olives. She could have sworn he'd eaten them the night she'd dined at the Fairweather mansion.

He gestured to the room. 'Do you mind if I make a few adjustments?'

'Knock yourself out.'

He immediately shifted the cushions out of their perfect alignment and shook out her throw rug before casually draping it across the sofa. He took a decorative rock from the mantel and placed it on the coffee table, pushed the platter of cheese and olives from the centre further towards one end. He moved the vase of fresh flowers she'd bought that morning to the end of the mantel, rather than dead centre, and then pulled a magazine and a book from the magazine rack, all but hidden by the sofa, and placed them on the little table by the door.

'There!' He dusted off his hands. 'Now the place looks lived in.'

Mia blinked. His few simple changes had made a big difference. The room now radiated warmth rather than stiff awkwardness.

Her hands went to her hips. 'How do you even know how to do that?'

He shrugged. 'You just need to relax a bit more, Mia.'

Relaxing around Dylan... Was that even possible?

She swallowed. 'I spoke to Carla through the week.'

'I know. She's talked of little else.'

Mia couldn't work out whether he was pleased about that or not.

'Carla's the reason I'm early. She seemed to think you might need a hand, and that I should be the one to offer it.'

He didn't smile.

She gestured to the room, trying to lighten the mood. 'Obviously she was right.'

He just stared at her, his eyes blue and brooding.

She pressed a hand to her stomach. 'I...uh... I think I have everything under control.' She kicked into hostess mode. 'Can I get you a drink? Beer, wine...soft drink?'

He chose wine. She poured wine for both of them and invited him to help himself to the cheese and olives. They sat there barely talking, barely looking at each other. Mia excused herself and pretended to do something in the kitchen.

They were rescued from their excruciating awkwardness when Carla and Thierry arrived fifteen minutes later.

'Oh, look at your cottage!' Carla gushed, hugging her. 'It's so quaint and pretty.'

Carla's kindness eased some of the burning in Mia's soul, and she could only give thanks that his sister's presence made Dylan a little more sociable. Thierry neither hugged her nor kissed her cheek. Not that she'd expected him to do either. He barely said hello.

The veal scaloppini was a melt-in-the-mouth success. The dinner, however, wasn't. Dylan complimented her on the food, made small talk about nothing of note, and every time Mia glanced at him a knife twisted into her heart. His despondency—his *unhappiness*—was her fault.

She hated it that she'd hurt him. And she didn't know how to make it right. More to the point, she didn't know if she *should* make it right.

Carla's eyes grew increasingly narrow as she glanced from Mia to Dylan. Thierry just continued to survey Mia with his usual and by now familiar suspicion.

She told a funny story about a wombat at Plum Pines but only Carla laughed.

She mentioned that she was considering getting a car and asked if they had any opinions on what she should buy. Thierry said he wasn't interested in cars.

Carla gaped at him. 'Liar!'

'I'm interested in *sports* cars. Mia can't afford one of those.'

'Don't be so rude!'

'No, Thierry's right,' Mia jumped in. 'I'm just after something reliable and economical.'

Dylan then subjected them all to a long, monotonous monologue about the pros and cons of a particular model of hatchback that had their eyes glazing over and Mia wishing she'd never asked the question in the first place.

'What is *wrong* with you two?' Carla finally burst out at the two men. 'I think it's brave of Mia to tell us the full story of her past. I don't care what the two of you think—it doesn't change the way *I* feel about her. She's been a lovely friend to me.'

'Carla, that's really nice of you.' Mia's heart hammered up into her throat. 'But I think you ought to know that Dylan doesn't have an issue with my past either.'

Carla folded her arms, her eyes flashing. 'Then what's the problem? What's wrong with the pair of you?'

'That's none of your business,' Thierry bit out.

'Dylan is my brother. Mia is my friend. Of *course* it's my business.' She turned to Mia. 'Is it because of that incident with the photographer?'

Dylan's hands clenched about his knife and fork. 'Why the hell did you have to tell Carla about that anyway?' he shot at Mia.

An answering anger snapped through her. 'I didn't know it was a state secret. Besides, I thought it only fair that Carla be prepared for the story to break.'

'I told you I'd take care of it!'

'You'll have to excuse my scepticism. I didn't know your reach was both long and powerful enough to stop a story that juicy from making the headlines.'

'There's a lot you don't know about me!'

He glared at her.

She glared back.

'Why did you wait until Tuesday night to tell Carla?'

The question ground out of Thierry, cutting through everything else.

Mia moistened her lips. 'Because I was afraid that once she knew the whole truth she'd despise me.'

Thierry leaned towards her. On her other side she felt Dylan tense.

'She *should* despise you.'

'Thierry!'

Carla's pallor caught at Mia's heart.

'Ignore him. He has a giant chip on his shoulder because his father was in and out of prison all through his childhood.'

Mia's jaw dropped as Thierry's animosity made sudden and perfect sense.

Thierry shot to his feet. 'I told you that in the strictest confidence!'

They all stared after him as he slammed out of the house.

Carla leapt up too, grabbing her handbag. 'I'll call you tomorrow,' she said to Mia, before racing after him.

Mia glanced at Dylan. Did *he* mean to slam out of her cottage as well?

He stared back, his mouth a hard straight line, and she realised he meant to do no such thing.

She swallowed. 'Dessert?'

'Please.'

Before Mia could retrieve the crème-brûlées the cottage phone rang. That phone hardly ever rang.

She lifted the receiver. 'Hello?'

'This is Andrew Fairweather, Ms Maydew—Dylan and Carla's uncle. Perhaps you remember me?'

His tone of voice said, *Of course you remember me.*

'Yes, sir, I do.'

'A disturbing report has reached me claiming that you and my nephew are romantically involved. Well?'

His tone reminded her of her father. Her hands trembled. *You stood up to your father.*

She pushed her shoulders back. 'No comment.'

'I know about your background, young lady!'

Her fingers tightened about the receiver. 'I can't say as I'm surprised.' She glanced at Dylan to find him watching her closely.

'I'm giving you a friendly warning.'

Oh, yes—very friendly.

'Stay away from my nephew and niece or you *will* be sorry.'

'I'll keep that in mind.'

The line went dead. She dropped the receiver to the cradle and made for the kitchen.

'Was that the press?' Dylan demanded.

She set a crème-brûlée in front of him and slid into her seat. 'Have a taste.'

He looked as if he wanted to argue, but he spooned some of the dessert into his mouth and an expression of bliss spread across his face. He swore—just a little swear word—in an expression of wonder, not of alarm or anger. 'This is *amazing.*'

She stared at him, her chest clenching and unclenching, her skin going hot and cold, and something inside her melted so fast she wanted to cry out loud at the shock of it.

She loved him.

She loved him utterly, but she couldn't see how things between them could ever work out.

'Mia?'

She straightened. 'It wasn't the press on the phone, Dylan. It was your uncle.'

Dylan swore—one of the rudest words he knew.

Mia flinched. For all that she'd been to jail, she was no hardened criminal.

'I'm sorry. I shouldn't have said that.

She waved his apology away. 'It doesn't matter.'

It *did* matter. She deserved better. 'He warned you off?'

'Yes.'

He set his spoon down. 'What did he threaten you with?'

Her lips lifted a fraction. 'It wasn't a threat, but a "friendly warning".'

As if that were somehow different! He wished to God he could smile with her, but his sense of humour had deserted him. It had abandoned him when he'd walked away from her last week.

Fear had taken its place. Fear that he would never find a way to win her love.

'And it wasn't specific—just a general warning to stay away from you and Carla or I'd be sorry.'

'Are you going to heed him?'

She picked up her spoon and pressed it gently to the crust of her crème-brûlée until it cracked. 'Surely you and Carla have some say in the matter?'

He stilled. That felt like progress. 'You're not going to buckle under to his bullying?'

'Your uncle reminds me of my father. I stood up to my father and the world didn't come crashing down. Mind you—' her sigh arrowed into his chest '—it didn't do me any good either.'

The smile she sent him made his eyes burn.

'I suspect that if he chooses, your uncle could cause trouble for me.'

'And all you want is a quiet life?'

She lifted her eyes heavenward. 'I *crave* a quiet life.'

Life with him would never be quiet.

She brought her spoon down on top of her dessert again, shattering the toffee crust further. 'But me standing up to your uncle isn't going to be enough for you, Dylan, is it?' She met his gaze, her eyes troubled. 'You want more from me, and I don't know if I can give it to you.'

He straightened *I don't know* was a monumental improvement on *No chance at all.*

'You want our relationship to become physical, and you assure me you can keep that news under wraps from the press. I'm even starting to believe you. But can you promise me—?'

He leaned across and pressed a finger to her lips. 'First things first.' He needed to remove a significant problem before focusing on the reasons behind her softening. 'You think my uncle can cause problems for you at work with Gordon?'

'The thought has crossed my mind.' She stabbed the spoon into her dessert. 'I liked my plan—gain a useful qualification that'll keep me in employment—but I think it's time to say goodbye to it.'

He removed the crème-brûlée from her grasp and placed

it out of reach before she totally mangled it. 'You have a new plan?' Even though he knew it was a long shot, he couldn't help hoping he featured in this Plan B of hers.

'I think I'd better start looking for unskilled work—factory work or waitressing. At a pinch I suppose I could join the fruit-picking circuit.'

A hand reached out and wrung his heart. *'No!'*

Her raised eyebrow told him he had no say in the matter.

'I *won't* leave you worse off than I found you. I *won't* be responsible for that.'

Too late.

The words whispered through him, leaving a bitter aftertaste. 'I promise to do everything in my power to ensure you keep your job at Plum Pines.'

He could see that while she believed the sincerity of his intention she didn't think he'd be able to achieve the desired outcome. She had a point. His uncle held a lot of sway.

He drummed his fingers on the table. 'Right. If that doesn't work… Look, I know you don't want to work for FWE, but you could still do a traineeship with the company.' He drummed his fingers harder as his mind raced. 'I'd put you under one of my managers. You'd hardly see me. Our paths would barely cross.' He'd make sure they didn't if it would help her accept his offer. 'After two years of working for FWE, you could get a job anywhere in the industry. Job security would never be an issue for you again.'

'Dylan, I—'

He held up his hand. 'This is only a fall-back plan, in case you're fired from Plum Pines. I don't want to be responsible for you losing your job. Ever since I've met you, all I've done is cause you trouble.' He started to tick off the list on his fingers. 'Gordon tried to fire you for flirting with me, when I was the one doing the flirting. I introduced you to Thierry, who tried to play the heavy with you. Felipe put you in an untenable position when he snapped that photograph. The press have tried to go to town on you. And now my uncle has threatened you. It's not a list to be proud of.'

She glanced away. When she turned back, her eyes were dark and troubled. 'I fear you're paying for it too, though,' she said.

She was worth any price he had to pay. Which would be fine if he were the one paying the piper and not her. When he looked at the facts baldly, he'd done nothing but cause her trouble.

'That really is quite a list.' For the briefest of moments her eyes twinkled. 'It hasn't been all bad. You've bought me chocolate, and I've had my toenails painted. And I got the opportunity to see some amazing art.'

It was a paltry list in comparison.

She pressed her hands together. 'Most importantly, though, we now know Thierry isn't mistreating Carla.'

That *was* something. He'd never have found that out if it weren't for Mia.

'I've also learned some decorating tips and had the opportunity to cook veal scaloppini. What more could a girl want?'

A whole lot more!

He dragged a hand back through his hair. 'Dinner tonight was truly awful. Not the food,' he added quickly. 'The atmosphere.' And that had mostly been his fault too.

Mia pleated the tablecloth. 'I thought you were sulking.'

He couldn't seem to find any middle ground where she was concerned. 'I've been trying to give you some space, but the effort is killing me.'

As soon as he said it he knew the admission was too much. Mia sat further back in her seat. Further away from him. He had to swallow a groan at the pain that cramped his chest.

Pulling in a breath, he forced himself to focus on the important topic of their conversation. 'Please tell me that if you do lose your job you'll allow FWE to employ you. I can't stand the thought of bringing that much trouble to your door.

I know it means working in events management, rather than in conservation, but once you've gained the qualification you can arrange your working hours so you can study at night for a different qualification if you want. If I'm reading you correctly, it's job security that's really important to you.'

She was silent for several long moments, but eventually something in her shoulders unhitched. 'Okay.'

He stared at her. 'You mean it?'

'I'm really, *really* hoping I don't lose my position at Plum Pines.'

'We'll call that Plan A.'

'But if I do lose it, then, yes... I'd like to accept your offer of a position at FWE. We can call that Plan B'

'You'll trust that I won't try and take advantage of the situation?'

She nodded, and he found that he could smile. If she trusted him that far...

He rubbed his hands together. 'I feel we're making progress.'

'Progress?' The word squeaked out of her. 'How?'

He leaned towards her. 'I want to throw our ground rules out the window, Mia. I thought I only wanted an affair with you—fun, pleasure, satisfaction.'

At each word her eyes widened.

'But I was wrong. I want a whole lot more than that. I want—'

She pressed her fingers to his lips before he could tell her he loved her. Her throat bobbed convulsively. 'You're moving too fast for me.'

He pressed a kiss to her fingers before wrapping her hand in his. 'I'll slow down.'

'Do you even know how to do that?'

'I'll learn.'

Her brow creased. 'Dylan, I can't promise you anything.'

'I know. I might have hope, but I don't have any expectations. I have no right to expect anything from you.'

Dark eyes stared into his. 'You have so much faith in me, and I have so little in myself.'

She had to find that faith or there'd be no chance for them. They both knew that.

Her gaze drifted down to his mouth. Her eyes darkened and her lips parted, as if she couldn't get enough air into her lungs.

'And yet your beauty continues to addle my brain,' she murmured, almost to herself. 'That can't be good.'

An answering desire took hold of him, his stomach muscles tightening and his skin tingling. 'I think it's excellent.'

She moistened her lips, her chest rising and falling. 'Would you like to stay the night?'

For a moment he couldn't breathe. His free hand clenched and then unclenched, before clenching again. 'I would *love* to stay the night, but you told me sex wouldn't make a difference.'

Her mouth opened, but no sound came out.

'Can you promise me that it *will* make a difference, Mia?'

Her gaze slid away and she shook her head.

He pulled in a breath and held strong. 'I want more than crumbs from you. I want everything.'

She looked as if she wanted to run away. 'I'm sorry. That was stupid of me. Especially when I just asked you to slow down.' She rubbed her brow. 'We should bring this evening to a close and you should say goodnight.'

He rose, forcing her to rise too. If he didn't leave soon he'd be in danger of settling for anything, however small. 'It's a hostess's duty to escort her guests to the door.'

She bit back a smile as he pulled her along in his wake. 'You're just angling for a kiss.'

He backed her up against the wall. 'It excites me to know you're burning for me.'

Her breath hitched. 'You promised slow.'

'It's just a kiss, Mia.'

'Nothing is *just* anything with you, Dylan. We both know that.'

'Then tell me to stop.'

Her gaze moved from his eyes to his mouth. 'Just a kiss?'

He grinned down at her and shook his head. 'I mean to leave you *really* burning, Mia.'

Her eyes widened. 'I—'

He covered her mouth with his own, keeping the caress gentle until she relaxed beneath his touch, her lips moving against his, her mouth opening to him… And then, without warning, he deepened the kiss, intensifying it using his lips, tongue, teeth. His hands pressed into the small of her back until her full length was against his. He used every weapon in his armoury to assault her senses.

'Dylan…'

His name was a groan of need on her lips, and it nearly drove him mad. She tangled her hands in his hair, drawing him closer as she tried to crawl into his skin, inflaming him beyond endurance. He pressed her back against the wall, his hands sliding down over her backside, his fingers digging into her buttocks, pulling her up and into him, his need for her a fire in his blood.

She wanted him too. They could have each other and…

He eased away from her. Their eyes locked. He wanted so much more than this from her, but he knew that if she asked him to stay now, he would.

She pulled in a breath, as if reading that thought in his face. With something that sounded like a sob, she planted a hand to his chest and gently pushed him away.

'Go.'

CHAPTER ELEVEN

MIA BARELY SLEPT that night. She gave up trying just before dawn. So when Carla pulled up at the front of the cottage just after six a.m. Mia happened to be sitting on her front step, nursing a mug of coffee.

She stood and opened the front gate, ushered Carla through. Carla trudged up the path and collapsed on to the step, and Mia's heart clenched at the sight of her friend's red-rimmed eyes.

Then she noted the faint blue bruise on Carla's right cheekbone and a hot pit of anger burned in her belly.

She brushed her fingers beneath it, unable to stop her eyes from filling. 'Not Thierry?'

Carla's eyes filled too. 'No. He's a jerk, but not that much of a jerk.'

'Not Dylan.'

It was a statement rather than a question. Dylan would never strike a woman.

Carla gave a short laugh. 'I think he'd rather throw himself off a cliff than hurt a woman.' She glanced at Mia and rolled her eyes. 'I mean *physically* hurt a woman. From what I can tell he's broken his fair share of hearts. The fact you're up so early leads me to believe he's given *you* a sleepless night.'

Mia felt her lips twist. 'In this instance I believe it's safe to say I've returned the favour.'

Carla's attempt at a smile almost broke Mia's heart. She sat down and put her arm around Carla's shoulders. 'Your uncle?'

Carla rested her head against Mia's. 'Yes...' she whispered.

The swine!

They sat like that for a while, letting the early-morning peace seep into their souls.

A sigh eventually shuddered out of Mia. 'He hit you because of me, didn't he? Because you refused to end our friendship. I'm sorry I've caused trouble for you, Carla. You don't deserve it.'

Carla lifted her head. 'He hit me because I refused to obey him—because I'm choosing to live my life the way I see fit. And it's not the first time it's happened.'

Mia called him one of the worst names she could think of.

A giggle shot out of Carla, but she nodded in agreement.

'C'mon.' Mia hauled her to her feet. 'Have you had an *ounce* of sleep?'

Carla shook her head.

She led her inside and pushed her in the direction of the bathroom. 'Go wash your face.' She pulled a soft cotton nightie from a drawer and ordered her to put it on, then pulled the covers back from her bed. 'In.'

'Oh, but...'

'We'll make a game plan after you've had some sleep.'

Carla glanced at the bed. 'A couple of hours *would* be good.' She glanced back at Mia, biting her lip. 'I really, *really* don't want to see either Thierry or Dylan at the moment. I know it's asking a lot of you, Mia, but I just...'

'You want to sort through things at your own pace. That's understandable.'

'I'm tired of men thinking they know what's best for me, telling me what to do.'

'I'll take care of Thierry and Dylan if they show up.'

Carla climbed into the bed.

Mia pulled the covers up to her chin, squeezed her hand briefly. 'Sleep well.'

She fortified herself with more coffee and went to sit back out on the front step to keep guard.

Dylan showed up at nine o'clock.

He looked tired and haggard and her heart went out to him. She forgave him—a little—for her own sleepless night.

He collapsed onto the step beside her. 'I've been looking for her for a couple of hours.' He gestured to Carla's car. 'Thierry rang at seven. I thought she was with him. That's when I realised she was missing. I'm glad she's here.'

Thierry chose that moment to pull up behind Dylan's car.

'She's a grown woman, Dylan. If she chooses to spend the night elsewhere, surely that's her business? Not to mention her prerogative. I'm sure *you* wouldn't appreciate it if she sent out a search party whenever *you* didn't come home.'

He thrust out his jaw. 'She's not answering her phone.'

'Likewise.'

She said it as gently as she could, but Dylan's eyes narrowed, the irises going a deep sapphire.

Thierry charged up the path. 'I want to see her!'

'I'm sure you do.' She kept her voice calm. 'But the fact of the matter is she doesn't want to see either of you at the moment.'

'Me?' Dylan shot to his feet. 'Why doesn't she want to see *me*?'

'I believe the phrase was, "I'm tired of men thinking they know what's best for me."'

Both men's jaws dropped.

Dylan paced.

Thierry just stood there with his hands clenched. He glanced at the door.

'It's locked,' Mia said. 'And if either one of you has the slightest interest in her well-being you won't start banging on the door. She's asleep.'

Dylan halted his pacing. 'You put her to *bed*?'

'I did.'

Thierry rested his hands on his knees, his face grey. 'I don't know what to do. I've been such an idiot.'

Dylan leapt forward and grabbed him by his shirtfront and shook him. 'What the *hell* have you done to her?'

'If I have to get the hose out to cool the pair of you off, I will.'

Those blue eyes swung to her. She read the anger in them—and the indecision.

'Let him go, Dylan. Carla is perfectly aware that the two of you have her best interests at heart, but she's entitled to a time out whenever she needs one. She doesn't have to consult with either of you beforehand.'

Dylan stared into her eyes so intently it felt as if he was scouring her soul. Finally, with a nod, he released Thierry. 'Sorry.'

Thierry straightened his shirt. 'No problem.'

She glanced back at Thierry. 'I don't know what your argument was about last night, but if you're truly sorry—'

'I am!'

'Then I suggest you come up with an honest explanation for why you behaved the way you did, promise to do better in the future, and have a heartfelt and grovelling apology ready.'

His fists opened and closed several times. He nodded hard. 'Right.'

His earnestness almost made her smile. 'Flowers might help too.'

His chin lifted. 'I can come back?'

She knew she wouldn't be able to keep him away indefinitely.

'You can come back at four. I'm not making any promises. It's up to Carla to decide if she wants to see you or not.'

'Right.' He swung away and made for the gate. He halted when he reached it and turned back. 'Thanks.'

With a nod, he was gone.

Had Thierry just *thanked* her? Wow!

Both she and Dylan watched him drive away—Mia from her spot on the step, Dylan from where he stood in wide-legged masculine magnificence on her pocket of front lawn.

As soon as Thierry's car had disappeared, he swung back to face her. 'Okay, you can let me see her now.'

'I'm sorry, Dylan, but the same holds true for you too.'

'You have to be joking!' He stalked across to loom over her. 'You *know* I only have Carla's best interests at heart.'

She stood, using the step to give her a height advantage. 'Has it never occurred to you that all your big brotherly pro-tectiveness—some might call it *over*-protectiveness—could be a *little* stifling?' She uttered 'little' in such a way that he couldn't miss the fact that she meant *a lot*.

He gaped at her. 'It's my job to look out for her.'

'She's an adult. She can look out for herself.'

'Just because your family let you down, it doesn't mean that's the way every family works.'

He spoke the words in a voice so low and controlled it sent ice tiptoeing down her spine.

He held out his hand, palm flat, eyes glittering. 'Give me the key.'

Her heart quailed, because she suddenly realised what a betrayal he would see this as—her keeping him from his sister. She wanted to weep. She'd finally found the one sure way to distance him, and now that she had she didn't want to use it.

Give him the key.

She lifted her chin and forced steel to her spine. 'No.' Planting her hands on her hips, she leaned towards him. 'Carla doesn't want to see you at the moment. Go home, Dylan. Stop being a bully.'

His hands fisted and his entire body started to shake. 'I could take it from you by force.'

She folded her arms and raised an eyebrow. They both knew he wouldn't.

He swore and she flinched. He didn't apologise, but she didn't expect him to.

'A *bully*?' The word ground out of him. 'I can't believe you're lumping me in the same class as Thierry.'

The pain in his words cut at her. 'I *do* put you in the same class as Thierry. Thierry loves Carla—adores her. He'd lay his life down for her. I know you would too. It doesn't change the fact that Carla doesn't want to see either of you for the time being.'

His eyes blazed, but his face turned to stone. He turned and stormed down the path, leaving as she'd ordered him to.

The backs of her eyes burned and her vision blurred. A lump lodged in her throat. Whatever fragile link had bound them together had been severed, and she felt the pain of it deep down inside her. It tore at something she thought might never be fixed.

At the gate, he halted. His shoulders sagged. She hated it that she'd hurt him, but she readied herself for a different form of attack.

He came back, his face sombre, his eyes throbbing. 'I owe you an apology. I just acted like a two-year-old throwing a tantrum because he's been denied what he wants. But I'm worried about Carla.'

'I know.'

He clasped her shoulders. 'Is she okay?'

He stared into her eyes and she realised he meant to trust whatever she told him. Her mouth went dry.

'Mia?'

Her heart thudded, though she couldn't explain why. 'She's upset.'

'With Thierry?'

'I suspect so. But mostly with your uncle.'

Dylan's lips pressed together in a tight line. 'His car was at the house when I got back last night. It was late, so he was already in bed. He left after breakfast. We shared a few home truths. I don't think he'll be back. I told him that if he caused trouble for you at your place of employment you'd come and work for FWE. I don't think your job will be in jeopardy from *that* region, Mia.'

'I… Thank you.'

'I didn't know he'd spoken to Carla.'

It wasn't her place to tell him about his uncle's violence. 'I think that after some sleep, and some lunch and some talking, Carla will be fine. She just needs time to clear her head.'

He squeezed her shoulders and then released her. 'Okay.'

He really meant to trust her?

'Thank you for looking after her.'

'She's my friend. Of course I'm going to look out for her.'

His eyes throbbed into her. 'I don't mean to be a bully.'

It took all the strength she had not to reach out and touch his face. 'I know that too.' And he wasn't—not really. 'If you were really a bully you'd have taken the key from me by force.'

'You don't see it, do you?' he said.

A desolation that made her heart catch stretched through his eyes. Her mouth went dry. 'What don't I see?'

'I just harangued you, bullied you, all but emotionally blackmailed you, but you held firm. You chose to do what you thought was right rather than submit to my will. Do you still believe you're weak and easy to manipulate?'

She froze. 'I…'

The yard spun.

'I can't keep doing this, Mia.'

Her gaze speared back to his. 'What do you mean?'

'I love you.'

Her heart stuttered in her chest.

'You *know* I love you. With everything that's inside me. I'd do anything to win your love. But it's not enough, is it? You're still so far away. I lose myself and I get so frustrated… I start to yell and then I turn into a bully.'

'Dylan, I—'

He pressed his fingers to her lips. 'I love you, Mia. I want to have a life with you. But I won't bully you into that. If you ever come to me, I want it to be because you love me too.'

She did love him, but...

Confusion swirled through her and she couldn't make sense of the riot raging through her. The smile he sent her made her want to cry.

He leaned forward and pressed a kiss to her brow. 'Tell Carla if she needs anything to call me.'

She nodded.

He held her gaze for a moment. 'I mean to give you all the space you want, Mia. If you change your mind, you know where to find me.'

Fear clutched at her heart.

With a nod, he turned and strode away. This time he didn't stop at the gate.

Every step that he took away from her increased the ache in her chest tenfold.

Carla slept until noon.

'Did Thierry show up?'

'He did. So did Dylan.'

'What did he say?'

'Dylan said you're to call him if you need anything.'

'What did *Thierry* say?'

Oh. 'The man is half out of his wits with worry for you... and fear that you're going to dump him.'

'Good!'

'I told him to come back at four. I didn't guarantee that you'd see him. But if you really don't want to see him again he'll need to hear it from you.'

Carla bit her lip.

'Can things not be fixed?' Mia asked.

Carla folded her arms. 'I guess that depends on him. He wants to be all strong and solitary and untouchable—but that's *not* how relationships work. It's not how *marriage* works.'

Each and every one of those darts found their mark, although they hadn't been aimed at her.

Mia rubbed a hand across her chest, trying to ease the ache there. 'I believe he's sincere in wanting to make amends.'

'You think I should see him?'

She recalled the absolute happiness on Carla's face when she and Thierry had picnicked. 'I think you should give him a hearing. I think things can be patched up.'

The other woman tried to hide it, but she brightened at Mia's words. 'What about Dylan?'

'I think you should call him.'

'I meant what about *you* and Dylan?'

Oh. She glanced down at her hands. 'I don't know. I need to go somewhere quiet and think.'

'So there's hope?'

She met Carla's gaze. 'I *hope* there's hope.'

After a moment Carla said, 'I'm going to ring Dylan. I want Uncle Andrew charged with assault.'

Mia's head shot up, a fierce gladness gripping her. 'Good for you. Women shouldn't have to put up with violence at the hands of men.'

Carla twisted her hands together. 'It'll create a media circus, though.' She eyed Mia uncertainly. 'And the reason for our argument will come out—which means you'll be spotlighted in the media too.'

'Me?'

Carla reached out and took Mia's hand. 'I know how much you've dreaded the media getting hold of the story that you and Dylan are dating. If the thought of publicity freaks you out that much, I won't go ahead with it.'

Her heart thumped. She waited for dread and fear to fill her, but they didn't. *Why* wasn't she crippled with fear?

The answer came to her in an instant. Ever since she'd

been released from jail she'd thought that scandal and losing her job, losing the chance of the quiet life she craved, were the worst things that could happen to her. She'd been wrong. Watching Dylan walk away this morning—that had been the worst thing.

Very slowly she shook her head. 'It doesn't freak me out. At least, not much.' She met her friend's gaze. 'You have every right to slay your dragons. I'll help in any way I can.'

Carla wrapped her in a hug. 'Thank you.'

At four o'clock Mia let herself into the Plum Pines office. Sunday was one of the busiest days as far as the general public were concerned—lots of barbecues, picnics and viewing of the exhibits. It was a busy day for the volunteers who helped to run the wildlife displays too, but the administration of the reserve was a strictly Monday-to-Friday enterprise. Which meant she'd have the office to herself.

With a heart that pounded too fast, she switched on one of the computers and then pulled Felipe's memory card from her pocket. Swallowing hard, she retrieved the image he'd snapped of her.

It filled the screen. She flinched and had to look away.

It's only a photograph!

She glanced back and tried to study the picture objectively, but after only a few seconds she had to look away again.

Muttering something rude under her breath, she pushed out of her chair and paced across to the far wall. Hauling in a breath, she turned back to the image once more.

Her heart squeezed tight and her eyes filled. Felipe had captured something that attracted and repelled her at the same time. He'd captured something that both soothed and frightened her.

What was it?

In that photo her expression was so unguarded it made her head spin. Was it hope?

She moved back towards the computer monitor to study the image more minutely, biting down on her thumbnail.

Hope was part of it, but…

She reached out and touched the face on the screen.

That smile…

The emotion pulsing through the photograph was *joy*. It was so present she could almost feel the laughter wrap around her.

Joy? She'd spent so long feeling ashamed of herself, so determined not to repeat her mistakes, she'd forgotten. She'd forgotten she had a lot of good inside her too.

Her hands clenched and unclenched. She'd told herself that she couldn't have fun and hope and joy in her life because she didn't deserve them—not after the things she'd done.

But…

She'd made a mistake—a big one—but that mistake didn't have to define the rest of her life unless she let it. Her heart hammered against her ribs. She didn't need to shut herself away. She just needed to choose the right path… the right life.

She fell back into the chair, her cheeks wet. There wasn't a tissue in sight, so she dried her cheeks on the sleeves of her shirt and sniffed rather inelegantly.

'Right, then.'

She might as well start living that life right away.

She seized the phone and punched in a number.

'Felipe Fellini.'

'Felipe, it's Mia.'

'Mia, darling—what can I do for you?'

She told him.

After she'd hung up she pulled in a breath and rang Dylan. He answered immediately. 'Mia! Is everything okay?'

His caller ID must have given her away.

The sound of his voice made her throat dry and she had to clear it before she could speak. 'Yes.'

'I've spoken to Carla. Are you sure you're all right with the publicity that a suit against Andrew will involve?'

She nodded, and then realised he couldn't see her. 'I'm sure.'

There was a pause. 'That's a surprise.'

She nodded again, more to herself this time. 'Yes.'

'What can I do for you?'

'I was wondering...' She wiped a damp palm down her jeans. 'I was wondering if I could invite you on a date next Saturday night. There's something I want you to see.'

'Has this anything to do with Carla and Thierry?'

'No. It's to do with me.'

'What time would you like me to pick you up?'

Dylan's heart thumped when he knocked on Mia's door. All week he'd alternated between hope and despair. Hope that this was the new beginning with Mia that he craved. Despair that this would be her way of bringing things between them to an end once and for all.

She opened the door. For a moment all he could do was stare. 'You look stunning!'

She wore a scarlet dress with a shimmering satin bodice, fitted beneath her breasts. The skirt fell to her knees in a cloud of chiffon that moved as she walked.

She pushed a strand of hair behind her ear. 'You look very nice yourself.'

He was glad he'd worn a dinner jacket. Especially when her hand fluttered up to her throat, as if the sight of him made it hard for her to breathe. The smile she sent him, though, held a hint of shyness—like a girl on her first date.

This probably *was* her first real date in nearly four years. Tenderness washed over him.

After she'd locked the front door he held out his arm, ridiculously pleased when she placed her hand in the crook of his elbow. 'Your chariot awaits.'

For good or for ill, he had a feeling he'd remember tonight for the rest of his life.

'Where are we going?'

She gave him an inner-city address. He had no idea what was there, but he didn't ask any further questions. He'd let the evening unfold at the pace she chose for it.

Dylan glanced out of the car window. Light spilled from the industrial-sized windows of a warehouse. He opened his mouth to ask Mia if she was sure she had the address right, but closed it again when she lowered her window and waved a card at an attendant standing on the footpath. The attendant directed them to a parking spot in front of the warehouse's huge double doors—the doors were closed except for a smaller door inset into one of them.

He switched off the ignition and turned to her. 'What *is* this?'

'I—' She broke off and hauled in a breath.

That wave of tenderness washed over him again, threatening to crush him. He reached for her hand. 'Are you nervous?'

'A little.'

'Of me?'

'Yes.'

The word whispered out of her and something blossomed in his chest. *Hope.* And it took firm root. 'You don't need to be nervous about me, Mia.'

He was hers. All hers. He didn't tell her out loud that he loved her, but he pressed a kiss to her palm, knowing that if she wanted to see it his love for her would be written all over his face.

Her gaze travelled over him and her breath snagged, her gaze catching on his mouth. Hunger and need chased themselves across her face. An answering hunger roared through him.

'Oh!' Her hand tightened in his. 'You can distract me *so* easily!'

The grin inside him built. 'Excellent.'

'Before you distract me further, I want to show you something. And then I want to talk.'

'And *then* can I distract you?' He waggled his eyebrows.

She gurgled back a laugh. 'Perhaps. If you still want to.'

He'd definitely still want to.

Without another word, he pushed himself out of the car and went around to open her door. She took his arm.

'This—' she gestured to the building in front of them '—is something of a first. Felipe has been prevailed upon to give the people of Newcastle a preview of his up-and-coming Sydney show.'

Dylan's stared at her. 'Who prevailed upon him?'

She moistened her lips. 'Me.'

She had?

Before he could ask what that meant, Felipe came towards them, arms outstretched.

'Darlings!' He kissed them on both cheeks in flamboyant greeting. 'I'm honoured to have you as my guests. Come!'

Dylan's head whirled as Felipe gave them a personal tour of some of the most amazing photographs Dylan had ever seen—his commentary both entertaining and revelatory.

Dylan glanced at Mia. She'd contrived this for *him*? Because she knew he appreciated art and photography? His heart gave a giant kick. Nobody had ever arranged anything so perfect for him in all his life. It had to mean *something*.

'And this, darlings, is the *pièce de résistance*! The jewel in my crown.'

Felipe led them around a screen to an enormous photograph positioned on one of the warehouse's end walls.

Mia!

He took a step towards it and Mia's hand slipped from his arm. It was the photograph of Mia! Her joy, her laughter and her love greeted him from the wall and he almost stopped breathing.

His every muscle tightened. He swung back to her, hands fisted at his sides. He'd lost the ability to be charming. Everything had been stripped away except raw need. 'What does this mean?'

Mia glanced at Felipe, who put a key into her hand.

'Lock up when you're done.'

She nodded her thanks.

It was only then that Dylan realised they were alone in this magnificent space. The show had been for him alone.

Mia didn't speak until the clang of a door informed them that Felipe had left. She moistened her lips. 'Are you cross that I gave Felipe permission to use the photograph in his exhibition?'

'Cross? No.' He glanced at the photo again and searched himself. He didn't feel disappointment either. Only wonder. 'I just want to know what all this means.'

'It means I've finally realised you were right.'

She moved to stand beside him and gestured up at the picture, though he could only look at *her*—the flesh and blood woman.

'That *is* the person I should become. It's…' She met his gaze. 'It's the real me.'

Her admission stunned him.

'I've realised that I deserve to be happy. More to the point, I've realised I *want* to be happy. And I've realised that being a field officer and leading a quiet life *won't* make me happy.'

She glanced at the photo and then at him.

'*You* make me happy, Dylan.'

He stared at her, humbled by the vulnerability in her eyes.

'I… I couldn't be happy until I forgave myself for my past.' Her hands twisted together. 'I know I've hurt you, and I'm so sorry for that. Truly. I'm hoping I haven't hurt you so badly that you can't forgive me. I'm hoping—'

He didn't let her finish. He kissed her instead.

The shock of his assault made her wobble on her heels, but he wrapped an arm about her waist and pulled her close, steadying her. She wrapped her arms around his neck and kissed him back.

When he lifted his head her eyes glittered and her chest rose and fell. And then she smiled, and it was just like the smile in the frame behind her—full of joy and love.

'That felt an awful lot like a you-still-love-me-too kiss.'

He stroked his fingers down her face. 'I will *always* love you.'

She took his face in her hands. 'I promise I will look after your heart and be the best person I can for you.'

He stared into her eyes, humbled all over again. 'Nobody has ever made a more meaningful vow to me. I'll cherish it forever.'

A cheeky smile peeped out. 'Good, because I'm also going to ask you to give me a job. I quit Plum Pines yesterday.'

He gaped. She just grinned back at him, so delighted with herself that he had to laugh.

'I don't want to be a field officer, and I don't want to be an events manager either. I just want you to give me a regular office job so I can put myself through a psychology major at university. I want to be a counsellor.' She lifted her chin. 'I think I have something of value I could offer to people.'

He ran his hands up and down her back, revelling in the way it made her shiver. 'How about I gift you the opportunity for full-time study as a wedding present?'

She went very still and Dylan held his breath.

'You want to *marry* me?' she whispered.

Very gently he took his arms from around her and, gripping both her hands, went down on one knee. 'Beautiful Mia, will you do me the very great honour of becoming my wife?'

Tears shone in her eyes. When she nodded, they spilled onto her cheeks.

He rose and she threw her arms around his neck. 'I can't

think of anything I want more than to spend the rest of my life with you, Dylan.'

He laughed for the sheer joy of it, swinging her around. 'How does November sound? We have a wedding going begging. We might as well use it.'

She eased back. 'What on earth are you talking about? Carla and Thierry have made up and—'

'They flew out to Vegas yesterday.'

She gaped. 'No!'

'So… November is ours if we want it.'

An enormous smile spread across her face. 'It's…perfect!'

He glanced at the photo on the wall and then down at her. 'No, Mia, *you're* perfect.'

She touched his face, her smile radiant. '*We're* perfect. Together.'

He couldn't top that, so he kissed her instead.

EPILOGUE

CARLA AND THIERRY bundled Mia out of the limousine and whisked her straight inside the small marquee that had been set up especially for her benefit—to shield her from the press and allow her a chance to freshen up.

As they'd only driven from her suite at an inner-city hotel with glorious views of the harbour to Plum Pines Reserve—a drive of less than fifteen minutes—she didn't really see what kind of freshening up was required. Unless she was supposed to try and quieten the excited dervishes whirling in her stomach. She had no chance of stilling *those*. She wasn't sure she wanted to.

Perhaps she should try and tame the grin that made her face ache? But she had no hope—nor desire—to do that either.

Carla, stunning in her hot-pink bridesmaid's dress, crouched down to adjust Mia's skirts.

Mia laughed ruefully. 'I went overboard, didn't I? I look like an oversized meringue.'

'You look *gorgeous*.' Carla continued to fluff up the skirts. 'Your dress is *beautiful*.'

The moment Mia had clapped eyes on the confection of raw silk and pearl beading she'd fallen in love with it. Apparently when she had said that she meant to live life to the full rather than hide in the shadows she'd meant it.

She hugged herself. 'It *is* beautiful.'

'I can't wait to see Dylan's face when he sees you.'

Today, nobody could mistake Mia for anything other than what she was—the bride, the centre of attention, the belle of the ball marrying her prince.

Those dervishes whirled faster and faster. Her cheeks ached from smiling. She lifted her chin. She wasn't ashamed of her joy. She wanted to share it with everyone.

She turned to find Thierry surveying her with his now familiar unsmiling gaze.

He nodded. 'You look stunning.'

She wriggled with excitement. 'I *feel* stunning. I'm so happy I think I could float off into the atmosphere.'

For the briefest of moments Thierry smiled, and it tempered the severe lines of his face. When he smiled, she could see why Carla had fallen for him.

She touched his arm. 'Thank you for agreeing to give me away.' He hadn't hesitated when she'd asked. He'd agreed immediately.

'I'm honoured.' One shoulder lifted. 'I'm starting to think I'd do anything you asked of me.'

From behind him, Carla sent her a wink.

Thierry frowned. 'You're sure we're okay?'

She rolled her eyes. 'I swear to God, Thierry, if you apologise to me one more time we're going to fall out.'

He shuffled his feet. 'It's just… I'm really sorry I misjudged you.'

Given his background, and the hardships his father's choices had forced on his family, Mia couldn't blame him for his reservations where she'd been concerned.

'As I misjudged myself, I can hardly blame you for doing the same. But it's all in the past now, and that's where it'll remain. It's time to move on.'

That was her new motto and she'd embraced it with gusto.

She reached out to take Carla and Thierry's hands. 'You're my family now—my sister and brother. I can't tell you how fortunate that makes me feel.'

Carla's eyes filled. Thierry cleared his throat a couple of times.

Mia blinked hard. She would *not* ruin her eye make-up. She wanted to look perfect for Dylan. 'So that's a yes—we're *very* okay.'

On impulse, they all hugged—before Carla tut-tutted and said something about crushing Mia's dress.

Mia laughed at her fussing, but a wave of excitement somersaulted through her. 'Oh, is it time yet? I can't wait—'

The flap of the marquee flew open and Felipe appeared. He clasped his hands beneath his chin when he saw her.

'Radiant!' he pronounced, before whisking a compact from somewhere and touching a powder puff lightly to her nose. He kissed the air above her cheeks. 'Perfect!'

He pulled out his camera and snapped a couple of pictures.

She waggled a finger at him. 'Don't forget—those photos are mine and Dylan's. None are to mysteriously appear in an exhibition.'

'Cross my heart, darling. Besides, your dishy intended is paying me enough to make it worth my while.' He pouted. 'Also, he made me sign some awful form full of lawyer-speak.'

Mia laughed.

'I've been sent to tell you everything is ready.'

'Oh!' She clasped her hands together.

'Nervous, darling?'

'Excited.'

He squeezed her hands. 'I wouldn't have missed this for the world.'

And then he was gone.

Carla handed her a bouquet of pink and white peonies. 'Ready?'

A lump lodged in her throat. All she could do was nod.

Thierry held the flap of the marquee open to reveal the red carpet that would lead her to Dylan. Carla set off down the carpet first. Thierry made Mia wait until Carla was half-way down the makeshift aisle before stepping after her.

Mia was vaguely aware of the beautiful music playing, of the murmurs of appreciation from their wedding guests, but her focus was wholly centred on the man standing at the other end.

His blond hair gleamed golden in the sunlight. His broad shoulders and strong thighs were outlined to perfection in his tuxedo. His heart was in his eyes. He didn't try to hide it from anyone, and she wasn't sure she'd ever seen anything more beautiful in her life.

Awe rose up through her…and more happiness than her body could contain. It spilled from her eyes and onto her cheeks.

He took her hand. His throat bobbed with emotion as he swallowed.

'You're so beautiful you make my eyes water,' she whispered, not caring about her make-up.

He smiled down at her. 'You're so beautiful you make my heart sing.'

The celebrant cleared her throat. 'Ready?'

Mia smiled up at Dylan. 'Yes.'

The service was simple but heartfelt. The reception was the epitome of joy and elegance. Mia felt like a fairytale princess.

After the meal had been eaten, toasts made, the cake cut and the bridal waltz completed, Dylan took her hand and they sneaked outside to stand at the wooden railing overlooking the lily pond. Lights twinkled in the trees, glimmering across the water's surface.

Dylan took her face in his hands and kissed her. A sweet, gentle kiss that promised a lifetime of kisses.

'Happy?' he murmured, easing back.

'More than I ever thought possible.' She smiled up at him before glancing back towards the marquee. 'Has anyone ever told you that you know how to throw a fabulous party?'

'What can I say? I'm gifted.'

She gurgled back a laugh. 'Look.' She pointed to Carla and Thierry dancing. 'They look gorgeous together.'

Dylan snorted. 'Carla should've had a wedding like this! *Elopement?*' He snorted again.

Mia leaned back against him. 'You just love any excuse to throw a party.'

'What's wrong with a party?'

'Absolutely nothing. I adore parties. I'm especially loving this one.'

She bit her lip then, and glanced up at him again.

'Are you sorry your Uncle Andrew isn't here?' The man might be a miserable excuse for a human being but he was still Dylan's uncle.

'Not a bit. I'll be happy if I never clap eyes on him again.'

There hadn't been enough evidence to charge Andrew with assault against Carla, but the scandal hadn't done the older man any favours. Especially since a young intern who worked in his office had made similar allegations against him. He'd been suspended pending an internal inquiry. If found guilty he'd lose his job. His political ambitions would be nothing more than dust.

Mia glanced up into her new husband's face and knew Andrew wouldn't be making trouble for any of them ever again.

Dylan smiled down at her. 'The day I won your heart was the luckiest day of my life.'

She turned in his arms, resting her hands against the warm hard contours of his chest. 'I'm the real winner, Dylan. You made me believe in love again. You showed me the power it had to do good. Whatever happens in the future, I'll never forget that lesson.' She touched her fingers to his face. 'I love you. I'm going to spend the rest of my life making you very, *very* happy.'

She wondered if her face reflected as much love as his did. She hoped so.

'Want to know what would make me happy right now?' he murmured, a wicked light flitting through his eyes. 'A kiss.'

Laughing, she reached up on tiptoe and pressed her lips to his, telling him in a language that needed no words how much she loved him.

* * * * *